"Whatever made me think you would assume the mantle of a docile wife?"

Hannah drew in a deep breath and released it slowly. "I didn't promise to obey."

"I vividly recall your insistence the word should be deleted from our vows," Miguel acknowledged.

"We made a deal," she reminded him, all too aware of the circumstances that had initiated their marriage.

"So we did," Miguel drawled.

HELEN BIANCHIN was born in New Zealand and traveled to Australia before marrying her Italian-born husband. After three years they moved, returned to New Zealand with their daughter, had two sons, then resettled in Australia. Encouraged by friends to recount anecdotes of her years as a tobacco sharefarmer's wife living in an Italian community, Helen began setting words on paper, and her first novel was published in 1975. And animal lover, she says her terrier and new Persian kitten consider her study to be as much theirs as hers.

Don't miss any of our special offers. Write to us at the following address for information on our newest releases.

Harlequin Reader Service
U.S.: 3010 Walden Ave., P.O. Box 1325, Buffalo, NY 14269
Canadian: P.O. Box 609, Fort Erie, Ont. L2A 5X3

Helen Bianchin

THE MARRIAGE ARRANGEMENT

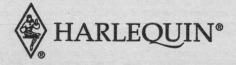

HARLEQUIN®

TORONTO • NEW YORK • LONDON
AMSTERDAM • PARIS • SYDNEY • HAMBURG
STOCKHOLM • ATHENS • TOKYO • MILAN • MADRID
PRAGUE • WARSAW • BUDAPEST • AUCKLAND

ISBN 0-373-12187-3

THE MARRIAGE ARRANGEMENT

First North American Publication 2001.

Copyright © 2001 by Helen Bianchin.

Visit us at www.eHarlequin.com

Printed in U.S.A.

CHAPTER ONE

THE grey skies held a heavy electric potency that threatened to unleash cacophonous fury at any moment.

Hannah turned on the car's lights, and flinched as a fork of lightning rent the skyline, followed seconds later by a roll of thunder.

She could almost smell the imminent onset of rain, and seconds later huge drops hit the windscreen in a rapidly increasing deluge that soon made driving hazardous.

A muttered curse escaped her lips. *Great.* A summer storm during peak-hour traffic was just what she needed. As if she weren't already late, with available time minimising by the second.

Miguel *would* be pleased at the delay, she decided grimly.

Almost on cue, her cell-phone rang, and she activated the speaker button.

'Where in *hell* are you?' a slightly accented male voice demanded with chilling softness.

Speak of the devil! 'Your concern is overwhelming,' she returned with silk-edged mockery.

'Answer the question.'

Rain sheeted down, reducing visibility to a point

where she felt cocooned in isolation. 'Caught in traffic.'

There were a few seconds' silence, and she had a mental image of him checking his watch. '*Where*, precisely?'

'Does it matter?' A resort to wicked humour prompted her to add, 'I doubt even you can organise some way to get me out of here.'

Miguel Santanas was a law unto himself, with sufficient wealth and power to command anyone at will.

Andalusian-born, he'd been educated in Paris, and spent several years based in New York managing the North American arm of his father's business empire.

'You could have closed the boutique early, missed the worst of traffic, and been home by now,' Miguel said drily, and she felt anger begin to stir.

The boutique was *hers*. She'd studied art and design, worked in fashion houses in Paris and Rome, only to walk out on a disastrous love affair three years ago and return home. Within months she'd leased premises, stocked the boutique with exclusive designer wear, and at the age of twenty-seven she had built up an exclusive clientele.

'I doubt one of my best clients would have appreciated being shoved out the door,' she returned with marked cynicism.

'Whatever made me think you would assume the mantle of a docile wife?' Miguel offered in a musing drawl.

She drew in a deep breath and released it slowly. 'I didn't promise to *obey*.'

'I vividly recall your insistence the word be deleted from our vows.'

'We made a deal,' she reminded, all too aware of the circumstances that had initiated their marriage.

Two equally prominent, independently wealthy families whose fortunes were interwoven in an international conglomerate. What better method of cementing it and taking it into the next generation than to have the son of one family marry the daughter of the other?

It had taken subtle manipulation to entice the son to relocate to Melbourne from New York, whereupon an intricate strategy had been put in place to ensure Miguel and Hannah were frequent guests at a variety of social functions.

The master parental plan had involved anonymous tips to the media, whose printed speculation had seeded the idea and waived the need for further familial interference.

Hannah, tiring of dealing with some of the city's eligible and not-so-eligible bachelors bent on adding her wealth to their own, was not averse to the security marriage offered, with the proviso she continued to maintain her independence. *Love* wasn't an issue, and it seemed sensible to choose a husband with her head, rather than her heart.

Despite the family business connection, ten years' difference in age, his boarding-school education both in Australia and overseas ensured their paths had rarely met, and she had been only eleven when he'd transferred to New York.

'So we did,' Miguel drawled. 'Have you reason to complain, *amante*?'

'No,' she responded evenly.

Miguel was an attractive man, whose strong masculine features and tall broad-shouldered frame portrayed a leashed strength emphasised by a dramatic mesh of latent sensuality and an animalistic sense of power.

At thirty-seven, he echoed his eminent success in the business arena in the bedroom. She hadn't known his equal as a lover. And wouldn't want to, she added mentally, for he satisfied needs she hadn't been aware existed.

Even thinking about his lovemaking made her nerve-ends curl, and sent heat flaring through her veins.

A sudden horn-blast alerted her attention as the car in front inched forward, then came to a halt.

In the distance she heard the wail of a siren, soon joined by another, and her stomach twisted as she envisaged the probability of a car crash up ahead, the twisted metal, the resultant injuries.

'I think there's been an accident,' Hannah revealed quietly. 'It might take a while for me to get through.'

'Where are you?' Miguel demanded.

'On Toorak Road, about a mile from home.'

'Drive carefully. I'll phone Graziella and tell her we'll be late.'

'Do that,' she responded with dulcet charm. It wouldn't create a drama if they arrived fifteen minutes after the specified time. Their hosts were known to allow up to an hour for their guests to mix and mingle before serving dinner.

The lights changed, and Hannah offered a silent prayer in thanks as the traffic began to move slowly forward.

The Deity, however, was not in a benevolent mood, and consequently it was almost six when she turned into the leafy avenue leading to the remote-controlled gates guarding entrance to Miguel's spacious double-storeyed home.

Landscaped gardens and manicured lawns provided a perfect background for an imposing residence set back from the road. Spanish in design, with thick cream-plastered walls, high arched windows, and a terracotta-tiled roof.

Hannah urged the white Porsche up the curved driveway at speed, and brought the vehicle to a swift halt beneath the wide portico.

Heavy panelled double doors opened the instant she slid from behind the wheel, and she spared the housekeeper Miguel employed a warm smile as she entered the foyer.

'Thanks, Sofia.' It had saved her fumbling for her key and bypassing the security alarm system. 'Would you mind asking Antonio to garage my car?' Sofia's husband took care of the grounds and the cars while Sofia tended to the meals and the house five days out of seven.

'Miguel is already upstairs?' At Sofia's verbal affirmative, she moved quickly towards the wide curving stairs leading to the upper floor.

Seconds later she gained the semi-circular gallery bounded by ornately designed balustrades. Five bedrooms, each with *en suite*, plus a large informal sitting room comprised the upper level. Original paintings were strategically placed on the walls, and there were occasional tables, magnificent ceramic urns and artefacts set in majestic splendour along the entire gallery.

The main bedroom was situated at the front of the house, and she moved quickly towards it, freeing the buttons on her jacket with one hand while slipping off one heeled shoe with the other.

Seconds later she entered the spacious bedroom with its elegant furniture and separate walk-in robes.

Miguel was in the process of fixing a cuff-link, and she took in the look of him, his stance, the superbly tailored trousers, white shirt, his broad, chiselled features, and the dark well-groomed hair.

Beneath his sophisticated façade there lay the heart of a warrior. Compelling, dangerous, she added silently.

At that moment he glanced towards her, caught her expression, and raised one eyebrow in silent query.

Eyes so dark, they were almost black, met hers, and she fought to control the way her blood coursed through her veins like quicksilver.

Was he aware how he affected her? Sexually, without a doubt, she acknowledged wryly. He had the touch, the skill, to turn her into a mindless wanton, for in his arms she lacked the power to be anything else.

Get a grip, she mentally chastised as she crossed towards her wardrobe.

'Twenty minutes?' Hannah intimated, extracting a black knee-length gown with a fine lace-patterned overlay. Stiletto-heeled black shoes, sheer black stockings. The effect would be understated style, and offset her honey-coloured skin and blonde hair.

'Try for fifteen.'

She made it in just under twenty, emerging into the bedroom freshly showered, dressed, her make-up complete. It took only minutes to step into her gown and close the zip fastener, then add minimum jewellery.

'Done.' She caught up an evening purse, and offered Miguel a sparkling smile. 'Shall we leave?'

Together they traversed the gallery and began descending the stairs. Even though she was in heels, her head barely topped his shoulders.

'New perfume?'

Hannah met his faintly quizzical expression and matched it with one of her own. 'A woman's weapon,' she asserted solemnly, and suppressed the feather-light shiver that slid across the surface of her skin as Miguel reached out and traced a slow finger along her collar-bone.

'You have no need of one.'

Her smile tilted the edge of her mouth. 'Are you seducing me?'

One eyebrow arched, and his teeth gleamed white as he slanted her a teasing look. 'Am I succeeding?'

Oh yes. But she wasn't about to tell him so. 'We have a dinner party to attend, remember?'

His husky chuckle almost undid her. 'Anticipation, *querida*,' he drawled. 'Is a game lovers play.'

'Is that how you regard our marriage?' Hannah queried lightly. 'As a game?'

Together they crossed the splendid foyer and made their way along a hallway leading to the internal garage.

'You know better than that.'

'Do I?' The words slipped out before she thought to stop them.

'You want I should show you?' Miguel countered with silky indolence as he paused to face her.

'I imagine you will, later.'

There was something in her voice, some indefinable quality that caused his eyes to narrow slightly and search for something beyond her carefully composed features.

She possessed a vulnerability beneath the sophisticated façade, a genuine empathy that held no artifice. A rare trait among the women of his acquaintance. He doubted she was aware he could define each tone of her voice, every expression, no matter how fleeting.

Tonight, for whatever reason, she was on edge, and he sought to alleviate it a little.

He lifted a hand and cupped her nape, tilting her head, then he covered her mouth with his own in an evocative tasting that brought forth a faint sighing sound as she leaned into him and kissed him back.

How long did it last? Seconds, *minutes*? She had no sense of time, only the feeling of regret as he broke contact.

His eyes were dark, unfathomable, and she was conscious of every breath she took, each beat of her heart as it thudded in her breast.

'There's a difference between sex and lovemaking, *mi mujer*,' Miguel said gently. 'You might do well to remember it.' He smoothed the pad of his thumb along the lower curve of her lip, and proffered a faint smile. 'You have no lipstick.'

Hannah gathered her wits together quickly. 'While you, *hombre*, have a mouth rimmed with *hazelnut noisette*.' She considered him carefully. 'It's not a good look.'

He laughed, a soft, deep, husky sound that curled round her heart and tugged a little. 'Minx. I don't suppose you have a tissue in that minuscule bag you carry?'

'Of course,' she said solemnly, extracting a tissue and handing it to him. 'I am always prepared for any eventuality.'

He used the tissue and discarded it, deactivated the car alarm, then unlocked the door and she slid into the passenger seat. Restoring colour to her lips took only seconds, and it was done by the time Miguel slipped behind the wheel.

Minutes later he eased the powerful Jaguar towards the remote-controlled gates, picking up speed as he gained the street.

Summer daylight saving time bathed their surroundings with a soft golden glow, and while the heat of the day still hovered it was offset by the car's air-conditioning.

The rain-storm had passed, the wet bitumen the only evidence of its brief intensity.

'Who are our fellow guests? Do you know?' Hannah queried idly.

'Forewarned is forearmed?' Miguel posed as he paused at an intersection, and she offered him a faintly wry smile.

'Something like that.' There were a few socialites of her acquaintance who delighted in setting a cat among the pigeons, then observing the result. It was very cleverly orchestrated, and provided amusing entertainment to the perpetrators.

A few years ago *she* had been an object of their speculation. Gossip, she amended, was unavoidable, but she detested any deliberate attempt to hurt or offend.

'Graziella mentioned Angelina and Roberto Moro, Suzanne and Peter Trenton,' Miguel relayed, shooting her a quick glance as the lights changed and traffic began to move. 'Esteban also has an invitation.'

Two partners in a prominent law firm and their wives, Hannah mused, together with Miguel's widowed father.

The del Santos invariably invited between ten and fourteen guests to share their table, and rarely revealed the identity of everyone attending. Graziella always commented that it made the evening interesting.

Hannah wondered who Graziella had invited to partner her charming father-in-law. A widow? Perhaps a divorcee?

'Is there any earth-shattering news I should be aware of?' Hannah queried as the car cleared another intersection.

'In the need to conduct scintillating conversation?'

Hannah bit back a wry retort. 'It negates any nasty little surprises.'

'Such as?'

'The fall of a prominent businessman due to tax avoidance. His wife cranked up her credit card in several élite boutiques.'

Miguel spared her a sharp look. 'Yours was one of them?'

'You got it in one.' It wasn't a fortune, she could write off the loss, but it left a nasty taste in her mouth that someone she trusted had deliberately ripped her off.

'Leave it with me.'

Resentment flared. 'I can handle it.'

'You don't need to,' he responded smoothly.

Hannah wanted to hit him. 'My business,' she said firmly. 'My problem.'

It could wait, Miguel decided, aware that pursuing it now would only exacerbate the situation.

Kew was an old, well-established suburb with large stately mansions, and Miguel turned the car into a leafy avenue, then halted outside an impressive set of gates leading to Graziella and Enrico del Santo's imposing residence.

'We'll discuss this later.' The window slid down and he pressed the intercom, gave his name, then waited as the gates swung open.

'The responsibility is mine, the action *my* decision,' she insisted as he parked the car on a wide pebbled apron adjacent the main entrance.

'Independence in a woman is an admirable quality,' Miguel intoned silkily. 'But there are times when you take it too far.'

He slid from behind the wheel, and she stepped out, then closed the door.

'And a man's indomitable will is a pain in the butt.'

'Pax,' Miguel slanted coolly, and she offered him a brilliant smile.

'Of course, *amante*,' Hannah offered in a deliberately facetious response. 'I wouldn't dream of tarnishing our image.'

'Behave,' he admonished as they mounted the few steps to the massive double entrance doors.

They swung open as they reached them, and a tall well-built man in his fifties offered an affectionate greeting.

'Hannah.' Enrico leant forward and pressed his lips lightly to one cheek, then the other, and pumped Miguel's extended hand. 'Come through to the lounge.'

As they drew close it was possible to hear the light hum of conversation, and Enrico led them into a large spacious room filled with heavy antique chairs and sofas grouped into comfortable facing sets.

Men stood, resplendent in formal dinner suits, and

each of the women resembled a model out of *Vogue*, the epitome in elegance and cosmetic perfection.

Hannah let her gaze skim a few familiar faces, her smile genuinely warm as she moved forward. She was one of them, born into established old money, educated and groomed to become part of an élite social clique. Hell, she'd even married into it.

Graziella enveloped them warmly, then she placed an arm through one each of theirs and drew them towards the centre of the room.

'You know most everyone. Except some dear people I very much want you to meet. They are visiting from Europe this summer.'

Graziella and Enrico had friends in almost every city in the world, and frequently entertained guests in their home.

'Aimee Dalfour, and her niece, Camille,' Graziella indicated in introduction. 'Hannah and Miguel Santanas.'

Camille was tall, slender, and startlingly beautiful, with hair that cascaded way down past her shoulders in a fall of lustrous sable. Exquisitely applied make-up, flawless textured skin, and a body to die for. Add a designer gown and shoes, expensive jewellery, and the result was drop-dead gorgeous.

'Miguel,' Camille purred in a sultry accented drawl. *'C'est opportune.'* She extended her hand and silently dared him to take it, her dark eyes simmering with blatant challenge.

This woman was trouble, Hannah decided with a sinking heart. Camille's fascination with Miguel was glaringly obvious. Also apparent was her intention to charm.

Hannah unconsciously held her breath as instinct caused all her fine body hairs to rise in protective self-defence, watching as Miguel brushed his lips to the manicured fingers, then released them.

'Hannah,' Camille acknowledged with pseudo politeness, and returned her attention to Miguel.

'Enrico will get you a drink,' Graziella informed them, ever the benevolent hostess. 'What would you like?'

Hannah was tempted to request something exotic, but she hadn't eaten since midday and then only a yoghurt followed an hour later by an apple. Alcohol on an empty stomach was not conducive to a clear head.

'Thank you. Orange juice,' she requested, and glimpsed Camille's faint *moue* at her choice.

'You don't drink?' she queried in a tone that indicated not to imbibe was a social *faux pax*.

Hannah inclined her head. 'In this instance I'd prefer to wait and have wine with dinner.'

'You do not have the head for it?'

Hannah chose not to rise to the bait, and merely smiled.

Minutes later she sipped the cool liquid from a stemmed goblet, aware Camille excelled in her role as temptress.

Keep it up, Hannah warned silently, and I'll scratch your eyes out!

At that moment Miguel placed an arm along the

back of her waist. A gesture that didn't seem to have
any effect at all.

The brush of beautifully lacquered nails as the
Frenchwoman touched Miguel's sleeve. The deliberately seductive smile. The promise lurking beneath
those impossibly long curled eyelashes.

Why, she was practically eating him alive!

Hannah decided enough was enough. She didn't
have to stand here and *watch* Camille's blatant seduction.

'If you'll excuse me?' She offered Camille a stunning smile, let it drift to settle on her inimitable husband for a few seconds before she moved away a few
paces to join her father-in-law.

'May I say you look beautiful tonight?' Esteban
complimented lightly as he leaned forward and
brushed his lips to her cheek.

'Thank you,' Hannah responded gently. 'It's a few
weeks since you've been to the house. You must have
dinner with us soon. We don't see enough of you.'

His smile was affectionately warm. '*Gracias.* But
you know how it is?' He gave a light shrug, and she
couldn't resist teasing him a little.

'A full social calendar,' she said gravely. 'And several women vying for your attention?'

'Ah, you flatter me.'

'No,' she assured him kindly. 'You're a very nice
man, of whom I'm very fond.' And one any woman
in her right mind would snap up in a minute. Except
his late wife Isabella held a special place in his heart,
and he had no desire to find a substitute.

A mutual acquaintance joined them, and after a few minutes she moved away.

'I think,' a light feminine voice suggested, 'you might need to sharpen your claws.'

Hannah turned towards Suzanne Trenton. 'Really? And use them on *whom*? Miguel?'

'*Camille*, darling. There are other methods a wife can use to tame her husband.'

It was meaningless repartee, spoken with jesting cynicism for the benefit of mutual amusement.

'Such as?' Hannah ventured, and Suzanne gave a soft laugh.

'Expensive jewellery.'

'Do enlighten me,' Miguel drawled as he threaded his fingers through those of his wife.

Hannah stood perfectly still for a few seconds, then she allowed her gaze to meet his. 'Pink and white diamonds,' she fabricated. 'A drop necklace and matching earrings.' A bewitching smile tilted the edge of her lips. 'They're quite beautiful.'

'Is this a wifely hint?' His mouth slanted into a humorous curve, at variance with the still watchfulness evident as he raked her features, noting the over-bright smile, her tense stance.

At that moment Graziella announced dinner was about to be served, and began directing guests towards the dining room.

'There was no need for you to desert me,' Miguel intoned mildly as they moved across the room.

'You appeared to be doing quite well on your own.'

'Careful, *querida*,' he drawled musingly. 'Your claws are showing.'

She gave him a winsome smile. 'Why, *amante*,' she offered with quiet emphasis, 'I haven't even begun to unsheathe them.'

If Graziella seated them close to Camille, she'd scream. The gods couldn't be that unkind, could they?

It appeared they could.

'I thought I'd place you opposite Camille,' Graziella remarked as she suggested prearranged seating arrangements. 'Hannah studied French and lived in Paris for more than a year,' she informed Camille graciously. 'As you're both in the fashion industry, you'll have much in common.'

Oh, my, this *was* going to be a fun evening!

CHAPTER TWO

'GRAZIELLA tells me you have a boutique on Toorak Road,' Camille began soon after they were seated. 'I must call in and check it out.'

'Please do,' Hannah said civilly, for what else could she say? Miguel was engaged in conversation with Peter Trenton, exploring the mores of legalese.

'Do you carry a range of accessories?'

A hired waitress began serving the first course, a delicate clear broth.

'A small selection of scarves, belts,' Hannah elaborated. 'Exclusive hosiery.'

Camille lifted an expressive eyebrow. 'Miguel has no objection?'

'To what, specifically?' she countered, reluctant to play Camille's game.

'Your little hobby.'

Considering the hours she worked, the responsibility to her clients, the sheer expertise required in running a successful business, the Frenchwoman's words were an insult...as they were meant to be.

Hannah summoned a sweet smile. 'He's relieved I have something constructive to do with my time.'

'Surely he would prefer you to be available for him?'

Hannah looked at the Frenchwoman, caught the avaricious gleam apparent, and opted for blatant honesty. 'On call to accommodate his slightest whim?'

Camille spread her hands expressively. 'Why... naturally, darling. If you don't, there are others who will oblige.'

'Such as you?' There was nothing like going direct for the jugular!

Camille appeared to choose her words with care. 'He's a very wealthy man, is he not?'

'And wealth is everything?'

Camille's smile didn't reach her eyes. 'It wields a power of its own.'

'A reciprocal power.' There was no need for pretence. It was no secret the Santanas-Martinez marriage had been conveniently arranged to legally combine two family fortunes.

'Power versus sexual attraction,' Camille pondered. 'Which would Miguel choose, do you think?'

Hannah held Camille's gaze, and discarded subtlety. 'I would say he already has.'

The other woman glanced at the wide baguette diamond wedding ring adorning Hannah's left hand. 'Most men will stray, given sufficient provocation.'

She wanted to dispute the words. Insist with total knowledge that Miguel was not *most men*, and his fidelity and loyalty to her were a given.

The soup plates were removed and a starter served. Hannah looked at the artistically displayed smoked salmon dribbled with a caper sauce nestling in a nest of finely cut salad, and felt her appetite diminish.

Tension curled inside her stomach, and she took a

sip of wine, then picked up her fork and attempted to do justice to the starter.

Miguel was an attractive man, possessed of a primitive masculinity that drew women like a magnet. There had been occasions when she'd been mildly amused by other women's attempts at coquetry, all too aware the flirtation was merely a harmless game.

Instinct warned her that Camille didn't fit into the *harmless* category, and that bothered her more than she cared to admit, for it raised questions to which she had no answers.

Could Miguel be tempted? Would he be sufficiently cavalier to indulge in an extra-marital affair? Somehow she didn't think so, but did she really *know*?

Theirs was a mutually convenient marriage that had *business* as its base. *Love* wasn't an issue...at least, not on Miguel's part. He cared for her, and she told herself it was enough.

One thing she was sure of—she wanted a relationship built on trust and loyalty. Not fabrication and empty excuses.

'Not hungry?'

Hannah turned towards her husband, met his steady gaze and glimpsed an indefinable quality in the depth of those dark eyes.

She summoned a light smile. 'Concern, Miguel?' His close proximity had a disturbing effect, for it made her aware of his exclusive brand of cologne meshing with freshly laundered cotton. His olive-toned skin was smooth, yet there was the hint of shadow despite the fact he'd only shaved an hour before.

'For you? Always.'

'Protecting your investment,' she ventured quietly, and caught the faintest glimmer of anger evident. So fleeting, she wondered if she'd imagined it.

'Of course,' he agreed silkily, and she tried to view the arrival of a superb paella with enthusiasm.

Camille seemed bent on engaging Miguel in conversation, and Hannah turned to the guest seated next to her and found herself caught up in an animated dissertation on the merits of boarding school education within Australia versus exclusive establishments overseas. Something which lasted until the paella was eaten, the plates removed, and a delicate seafood stew was served.

'Graziella mentioned you have an interest in the fashion scene,' Hannah ventured, in a bid to distract Camille's attention from Miguel.

'I model.'

Two words that supposedly said it all, Hannah reflected. 'Any particular fashion house?'

Camille proffered a haughty smile. 'Whoever offers the highest fee.'

'I was in Paris for the latest season's showing,' she mentioned conversationally, aware she hadn't seen Camille on the catwalks. Such striking looks wouldn't have escaped her notice, she was sure.

'I did Milan and Rome.' Camille lifted a hand and smoothed back a fall of hair in a gesture designed to focus attention on beautifully lacquered nails and her superb facial bone structure.

It had undoubtedly taken her hours to dress and perfect her make-up. Far removed from the nineteen minutes Hannah had allowed herself!

The main course comprised *pescado a la sal* served with a delicious salad, and she ate a small portion of the delicate fish flesh with contrived enjoyment.

'I believe we have a mutual friend,' Camille commented as Hannah finished the last of her salad.

It seemed possible, given their combined knowledge of the European fashion industry. 'I'm sure we have,' Hannah agreed as she lifted her goblet and took a sip of excellent white wine.

'Luc Dubois.' The name silvered the air, no less dramatic for its calculated delivery.

Hannah was conscious of a stillness at the table, as if all conversation had suddenly stopped...or was that just her imagination?

Her fingers tightened fractionally as she slowly set the goblet down onto the table. Miguel didn't move, but she could sense the flex of his body muscles beneath the expensive tailoring.

'Luc is not one of my friends,' she said quietly. 'He lost any claim to that distinction three years ago.'

The Frenchwoman arched an eyebrow in obvious disbelief. 'He particularly asked me to convey his regards.'

She could simply incline her head and retreat. Except such an action would play into Camille's hand, and there was something happening here that warned of a need for confrontation.

'I find that difficult to believe,' Hannah relayed evenly, aware that none of the guests spoke a word. 'We didn't part on good terms.'

'Really? He spoke of you in quite—' she paused deliberately, allowed her eyes to widen, and then appeared to choose her words ' — glowingly graphic terms.'

This was a calculated attack, and Hannah felt incredibly angry that Camille had chosen the verbal strike in public. To what purpose?

'Luc was a European playboy who preyed on any woman who could fund his expensive lifestyle,' Hannah relayed with a calm she didn't feel. 'I walked out on him as soon as I discovered he was a superficial leech.' She lifted her shoulders in a light dismissive shrug. 'End of story. The press made much of it at the time.' She even summoned a faint smile, albeit that it held a degree of cynicism. 'The Australian heiress and the French photographer.'

She held Camille's gaze. 'If you want all the details, I'm sure you could look it up in any of the media archives.' So be damned, she concluded silently. It was old news, past news, and her only regret was that she'd been very cleverly fooled by a practised master of deceit.

'Oh, dear,' Camille declared with a stab at contrition. 'I am so sorry. I didn't realise...' She trailed to a halt.

No, you're not, Hannah thought, and yes, you already knew. You just wanted to create an awkward situation.

Miguel covered Hannah's hand with his own, then he leaned towards her and brushed his lips to her temple. *'Brava.'*

His action deflated the air of tension, and within seconds everyone began talking at once.

Dessert was served, and Hannah forced herself to do justice to the *tocino de cielo*, a rich custard. She sipped excellent vintage wine, conversed with fellow guests, and gave every pretence of having a wonderful time.

She laughed at humorous anecdotes, commiserated with the Trentons at the difficulty of getting their two-month-old daughter enrolled into an élite private school, and attempted to ignore Camille's frequent slip in resorting to evocatively delivered French. Did the Frenchwoman imagine no one else understood? Or perhaps she didn't care if they did.

Miguel was fluent in French and Italian, as well as his native Spanish. Hannah had the advantage of the former two, but, even if she'd had no knowledge of the spoken word, the cadence of Camille's voice and its provocative delivery left little doubt Miguel was her target.

To his credit, Miguel did nothing to encourage the attention. But after almost three hours of observing the coveted glances, the blatant verbal seduction, Hannah was tiring of the pretence.

Smiling, when all she wanted to do was render Camille some form of injury. Her jaw *ached* from it, and her palms itched with the need to slap the Frenchwoman's face.

Coffee was served in the lounge, and she didn't know whether to laugh or cry with frustrated irritation when Camille wandered over to join them.

Dear heaven, the woman was persistent!

'It would be so—' Camille paused fractionally '—pleasant,' she stated, 'if you were to include me as a guest, socially.' She gave an expressive smile. 'My aunt, her friends...' She trailed off, and her slender shoulders lifted in a typical Gallic gesture. 'We have different interests, *comprendez-vous*?'

Hardly surprising, considering Camille's sole interest appeared to be Miguel!

'How long will you be staying?' Hannah asked, hoping the visit would be extremely short!

The Frenchwoman lifted an expressive hand, then let it fall. 'I have no immediate plans. A few weeks, several. Who is to say?'

'I am sure Graziella has made arrangements to entertain you,' Miguel drawled, and received a sultry smile.

'One must hope you are also included in such...' she trailed deliberately '...arrangements.'

Not if I can help it, Hannah decided as she endeavoured to subdue her anger.

Miguel took Hannah's empty cup and placed it with his own onto a nearby side-table. His expression was polite as he caught hold of his wife's hand and inclined his head towards Camille.

'If you'll excuse us?'

'You are leaving? It is so early,' the Frenchwoman protested.

'Goodnight,' Miguel bade smoothly, only to discover Camille didn't give up easily.

'You must both be my guests at dinner. Together with Graziella and Enrico, my aunt.' She paused, and offered a sweet smile. 'Miguel, you must bring Esteban.' She cast Miguel a deliberately seductive look. 'We shall make a date, yes?'

'We'll check our social diary and get back to you,' Hannah intimated smoothly, aware this was one engagement she had no intention of keeping.

Camille's expression didn't change, but Hannah glimpsed a brief malevolent gleam in those dark eyes, and felt the beginnings of unease.

Cynical bantering on occasion was part of the game a number of people played, for it formed amusing repartee. But instinct warned Hannah the Frenchwoman played by no one's rules but her own.

'Nothing to say, *querida*?' Miguel drawled as he eased the Jaguar out from the driveway.

She turned towards him, saw the beam of oncoming headlights cast angles and planes to his strong-boned features, and endeavoured to inject amusement into her tone.

'You expect me to *condone* Camille's blatant behaviour?'

'I could almost imagine you are jealous.'

He was amused, damn him!

'Am I supposed to answer that?' she demanded coolly.

He spared her a quick glance, caught the fiery blue glare aimed in his direction, then returned his attention to the road.

'It might be interesting to hear you try,' he declared indolently, and she burst into angry speech.

'What would you have me say?' Her fingers clenched over the clasp of her evening purse. 'That I objected to the way Camille monopolised your attention? *And* flirted outrageously.' She drew in a deep breath and expelled it slowly. 'Dammit, she has designs on you! Anyone would have had to be *blind* not to notice it!'

'Should I be flattered?'

'Are you?' She held her breath waiting for his reply.

'No,' Miguel declared with unruffled ease.

'Hold that thought,' Hannah said darkly.

'Why, *amante*?' he teased mercilessly as he gained the main street. 'What would you do if I succumbed to her charms?'

'Commit grievous bodily harm.' And die a little, she added silently. 'Then divorce you.'

He cast her a sombre glance. 'Extreme measures.'

'What would you do if I showed an interest in another man?' Hannah retorted, unable to resist taunting, 'Turn the cheek and look the other way?'

'I'd kill you.' His voice held a dangerous softness that sent shivers feathering a path down her spine.

'Wonderful,' she remarked facetiously. 'A few

hours in Camille's company, and we're not only arguing, we're threatening divorce and murder.'

The Frenchwoman was a witch, Miguel acknowledged grimly, and, unless he was mistaken, a very dangerous one.

'While we're on this particular subject,' Hannah continued, 'what importance do you place on Camille's deliberate mention of my *bête noir*?'

'Luc Dubois?'

'That's the one,' she conceded.

'Do you still retain an interest in him?'

'No,' Hannah declared vehemently. Even now she found it difficult to accept the Frenchman had penetrated her guard. *She*, who could tag a man's superficial charm in an instant, aware his main interest was her family's wealth, not *her*. Except Luc had been incredibly patient, known which buttons to push, and when. She'd fallen into his arms like a peach ripe for the picking.

'So sure, Hannah?' Miguel pursued silkily.

How could he ask that, when Luc didn't even begin to compare with the man who was now her husband?

'Yes.' She turned towards him. 'You have my word.'

'*Gracias.*'

'Such is the recipe for a happy marriage.'

'Cynicism doesn't suit you, *mi mujer*,' Miguel drawled.

'Ah, but I love this honesty we share. It is *très bonne*, don't you agree?'

'I can think of a more apt description.'

It didn't take long to reach their tree-lined street and traverse the driveway. Minutes later she followed Miguel indoors.

'Get the credit slips from your briefcase,' he instructed as they reached the foyer. At her puzzled look, he elaborated, 'The client who ran up debt all over town. I'll take care of it.'

'No, you won't,' she said emphatically. 'I can do it myself.'

'Why?' he queried steadily. 'When I can do it so much more easily?'

She flung him a baleful glare. 'Because I'm independent.'

'And stubborn,' Miguel added.

'No,' she disagreed. 'Self-sufficient.'

'Tenacious.'

'That, too,' she admitted, then allowed, 'If I have a problem, I promise I'll call on you.'

It would have to suffice, Miguel conceded. 'Are we going to stand here bandying words, or do we go to bed?'

She felt inclined to deny him. To turn her back and ascend the stairs alone. Yet to deny him was to deny herself. And she needed the reassurance of his touch, the possession of her body. To feel, in the darkness of the night, that she meant more to him than just part of his life as a convenient wife. To pretend for a while that the marriage was real, and what they shared was special, not just very good sex.

'Oh, *bed*,' she agreed. 'Definitely.'

'Minx,' he declared. 'What if I'm tired?'

'Are you?' she asked seriously, then wrinkled her nose at him. 'I wouldn't think of overtaxing your strength.'

He laughed, and the sound curled round her nerve-ends as he caught hold of her hand and led her upstairs. 'Let's see who cries *wolf* first, shall we?'

This, Hannah breathed shakily minutes later as Miguel slid the zip fastening free from her gown, was like entering a sensual heaven. He had the touch, the knowledge, the skill, to divine a woman's needs.

And fulfil them, she added with a silent gasp as the gown slid in a silken heap to the floor. The light brush of his fingertips trailed an evocative path over sensitised skin as he eased the silken briefs down over her thighs.

She stepped free of them and at the same time discarded the heeled shoes that added four inches to her height.

He was wearing too many clothes, and she pushed his jacket from his shoulders, tugged at his tie, then freed shirt buttons with restless speed.

His lips settled at the sensitive hollow at the edge of her neck, and sensation arrowed through her body as he used his tongue and his teeth to tease a tantalising kiss that had her arching towards him.

His shirt fell onto the carpet, and her fingers feverishly attacked the buckle on his belt, then tended to the zip on his trousers.

Miguel's contribution to shucking his clothes was to step out of his shoes and pull off his socks.

She reached for his briefs, and slid them free, awed

by the state of his arousal. It fascinated her that such a part of man's anatomy could drive a woman wild, and provide such pleasure.

Unbidden, she drew the pads of her fingers lightly over its silken length, caressing with a sense of captive thrall.

'*Amada,*' Miguel growled softly. 'If you don't want to be tossed down onto the bed and possessed without delay, I suggest you stop that *now.*'

She lifted her head and offered him an infinitely sweet smile. 'Why?'

He uttered a faint groan. '*Madre de Dios.*' The words left his lips in a rugged supplication as he dragged her close.

His mouth covered hers in a kiss that drugged her senses and tore at the very fabric of her soul.

Control, she had none. There were only the man, the moment, and an intensity of emotions so overwhelming she simply held on and joined him as he took her to the heights and beyond before free-falling down to a state of exotic warmth and satiation.

Her body felt like a finely tuned instrument that had been played by a virtuoso. Exultant, still clinging to the sweet sorcery of a master's exquisite touch.

She loved the feel of him, his sheer strength and passion, tempered by a control she sorely wanted to break. What would it be like to experience his unbridled lovemaking? To crash through the barriers of restraint and be taken with a raw primitive hunger that knew no bounds?

Dear Lord. Just thinking about it sent renewed heat

racing through her veins and had her moving restlessly against him.

His lips brushed her temple, almost as if he were attuned to the depths of her innermost needs, and his arms tightened as she found his mouth with her own.

This time it was she who nurtured his desire and sent it spiralling towards hungry passion in a mesmeric coupling that left them both slick with sensual sweat and fighting to regain a steady breath.

'Witch,' Miguel teased huskily as he buried his lips against her breast.

'Hmm,' Hannah murmured with bemused contentment, only to give a tiny gasp as he began teasing the tender peak, alternately with his tongue and the edge of his teeth, taking her to the brink between pleasure and pain.

Then with one fluid movement he slid from the bed, scooped her into his arms, carried her into the *en suite* and stepped into the large shower stall.

Seconds later warm water cascaded from four strategically positioned shower-heads, and Hannah slid to her feet as Miguel reached for the soap.

Evocatively sensual, they lingered for a while, then Miguel closed the water dial, snagged two towels, and once dry, they returned to bed to sleep.

Except after the first few hours Hannah was plagued by dreams that had her tossing restlessly until dawn, followed by a deep fitful sleep as light began filtering through the curtains.

She was unaware of the soothing touch of the man

who lay beside her, or that he curled her body close in to his more than once through the night.

Nor was she aware that he woke early, and propped himself comfortably on his side to watch her sleep.

She had delicate features, and the softest, silkiest skin of any woman he'd had the pleasure to touch, he mused gently. The tousled length of her hair lent an abandoned look, and her lashes were long, curling upwards at the ends. The mouth was lush, the lips softly curved in sleep. Capable hands, slender, displaying the band of diamonds and splendid pear-shaped solitaire that claimed her as his own.

She bore an air of fragility that was deceptive, for she possessed an inner strength, an innate honesty that decried artifice or deceit.

He would have liked to rouse her into wakefulness, to feather light kisses over every inch of her skin until she reached for him, then make long, slow love.

The generosity of her response never failed to move him, physically, mentally, emotionally.

Miguel felt his senses stir, and knew if he remained in bed she wouldn't sleep much longer. With a husky groan he rolled over and slid to his feet, then he walked naked into the *en suite* and stood beneath the shower.

CHAPTER THREE

HANNAH woke late, took one look at the digital clock and raced to the shower, then she dressed and applied basic make-up in record time before running lightly downstairs.

Miguel was in the process of draining the last of his coffee when she entered the kitchen, and heat flared through her veins at the mere sight of him.

It was as if she could still feel his touch, the masculine heat of his possession, the passion...

Dear heaven, she cursed shakily. This was post-coital awareness at its most provocative!

He looked at her and glimpsed the faint tremor that shook her lush mouth. Did she have any conception of her beauty? Something that went far beyond the visual, to the depths of her soul. At this precise moment she was remarkably transparent, and it moved him almost beyond measure.

He watched as she collected a glass and poured herself some fresh orange juice, then she plucked a slice of toast from the rack and spread it with marmalade.

'Why didn't you wake me?' Hannah queried in the quest for normality. She took a bite of the toast and followed it down with black sweet coffee.

He looked every inch the corporate executive, his

tailoring impeccable, a dark silk tie resting against a pristine white shirt.

'I reset the alarm,' Miguel relayed imperturbably, and checked his watch. 'Timed to go off around now.' He cast her a quizzical glance. 'Why don't you sit down?'

Hannah shook her head. 'No time.'

Dammit, he looked good. She wanted to slide her fingers through his hair, lower her head down to his, and kiss him until they both had to pause for breath.

Dangerous thoughts, she perceived as she took a long swallow of coffee. If she gave in to them, she'd be even later for work, and that would never do!

Instead, she finished the toast, downed the last of her coffee, then she extracted a banana and an apple from a silver fruit bowl, caught up her car keys and followed him through to the garage.

Miguel unlocked the door, and regarded her steadily over the top of the Jaguar. 'A restless night, no breakfast to speak of, and food on the run isn't an ideal way to start the day.'

She effected a light shrug. 'So I'll grab coffee and something to eat later.'

He wanted to wring her slender neck. 'See that you do.' He pulled open the door and slid in behind the wheel.

'Yes-sir.'

He shot her a dark speaking glance, freed the electronic garage mechanism, then he fired the engine and eased the car towards the gates.

Hannah's soft curse feathered the air accompanied

by an exasperated sigh. Work beckoned, and there was no time to dally if she was to open the boutique on time.

Seconds later she exited the driveway and headed towards Toorak Road, her mood reflective as she bore with morning peak traffic.

It would have been nice to have woken in Miguel's arms, stirred by his touch, enticed into sex by his passion in an early-morning ritual. She missed the shimmering sensual heat, the electrifying hunger followed by a languid after-play, for it was then they talked awhile before sharing a leisurely shower.

Camille's features sprang all too readily to mind, intrusive and vaguely taunting.

The power of pre-emptive thought? Hannah pondered as she dispelled the Frenchwoman from her mind and focused on the day ahead.

The courier service was scheduled to deliver some new stock this morning, and she mentally selected a stunning ensemble as window display, its accessories, and the rearrangement and placement of existing stock.

By the time she unlocked the boutique Camille temporarily ceased to exist.

Twice during the next hour her hand hovered over the phone. She badly needed to hear Miguel's voice, if only to say 'hi'. Discussing what lay ahead in their respective days had become an early-morning habit. Dammit, she'd ring and ask him to meet her for lunch. Cindy could manage the boutique for an hour, longer if necessary.

Without hesitation she keyed in the digits for his mobile phone, only to have the call go to voice-mail. She left her name and invitation, then busied herself with routine chores.

Cindy, a friend with a flair for fashion who welcomed part-time work while her daughter was in school, arrived at ten, closely followed by the courier.

Unpacking, checking invoices and preparing stock for display took time, and there were the serious clients who came to buy and not-so-serious passers-by who merely wanted to browse.

Then there were the phone calls, none of which was Miguel. Until eleven-thirty, when Hannah had all but given up on him.

'It's *the man*,' Cindy indicated as she extended the cordless handset.

Hannah moved a few paces away. 'I thought we might do lunch.' She drew a slight breath, then released it. 'I can get away any time between now and two.'

'I'm tied up with meetings all afternoon,' Miguel drawled. 'Can it wait until tonight?'

He sounded mildly amused, almost as if he sensed the reason behind her call. 'Of course.'

'*Hasta luego, querida,*' he bade indolently, and cut the line.

'Will you finish doing the window, or shall I?' Cindy queried seconds later, and Hannah gestured towards the clothed mannequin.

'Be my guest.' A cleverly draped scarf, an elegant brooch would add the final touches, together with heeled shoes and matching handbag. Something that would take only minutes to complete.

The end result was stunning, and Hannah was quick to add her compliment. 'Why don't you take a break for lunch?' she suggested, checking her watch. 'I can manage for a while.'

Most of the regular clientele chose to do their shopping mid-morning or mid-afternoon. For the most part, the time between midday and two was spent lunching at any one of several trendy cafés or restaurants in and around the city and its élite suburbs.

Cindy collected her bag and made for the door.

'See you soon.'

Hannah crossed to the CD player, removed the morning selection and inserted sufficient discs to provide soothing unobtrusive background music until closing time.

The electronic buzzer heralded the arrival of a prospective client, and Hannah turned with a welcome smile in place, only to have it momentarily freeze as she caught sight of Camille.

Tall, proportionately slender, the Frenchwoman exuded confidence and a degree of arrogance as she stepped forward. Dressed in designer clothes and wearing expensive perfume, she was elegance personified.

'*Bonjour*, Hannah.' She inclined a perfectly coiffed head, and scanned the carefully arranged racks.

'I thought I might visit.'

Somehow Hannah doubted *clothes* were Camille's main purpose. 'How nice of you to call in.' At what point did politeness cross the line and become a white lie? She indicated a rack of imported designer labels. 'Is there anything in particular I can help you with?' She crossed the floor and extracted a gown that would look stunning on Camille's tall frame.

'Darling, I can get that in Paris.' Her mouth pursed, and her eyes assumed a hardened gleam as she riffled through carefully spaced hangers with total disregard for their existing presentation.

Hannah watched as the Frenchwoman pulled out a hanger, examined the garment with disdainful criticism, then returned it carelessly back onto the rack before moving a pace or two and repeating the process.

There was little doubt as to the deliberateness of the action, and Hannah wondered just how long it would take for Camille to cut to the chase.

Exhausting garments displayed on one side of the boutique, the Frenchwoman crossed the floor and began a similar examination of various silk shirts.

'How does it feel being manipulated into a loveless marriage?'

Four minutes, give or take a few seconds, Hannah calculated. If Camille wanted to conduct a verbal altercation, then so be it. She met the woman's hard stare, and arched a delicate eyebrow. 'Manipulated by whom?'

Camille's gaze narrowed. 'It doesn't bother you Miguel's motivation was born out of *duty*? To his father, and the Sanmar conglomerate?'

Hannah took time to ponder the Frenchwoman's

words. 'For someone who has only been in Melbourne a short time, you seem to have acquired considerable information.'

'Graziella is very discreet. However, my interest in Miguel was captured several weeks ago at a party in Rome,' Camille enlightened with a secretive smile. 'Miguel attended briefly with a business associate.'

Hannah had instant recall. She'd flown in to buy new season's stock, tying the visit in with one of Miguel's Italian business meetings. She even remembered the evening in question, and a wretched migraine that had seen her creep into bed while issuing instructions for Miguel to go on to the party without her.

'I made it my business to discover everything about Miguel Santanas,' Camille continued relentlessly. 'His marriage, his wife, her background.'

This was far more complex than idle curiosity. Almost chilling, Hannah realised silently.

'And your affair with Luc Dubois,' the Frenchwoman revealed, intent on analysing Hannah's expressive features. 'Interesting man.'

Interesting didn't come close. The man was a practised rogue, and it still irked that it had taken her a few months to lose the fantasy and face reality.

'I imagine this is leading somewhere?' Hannah queried coolly.

'Of course, darling. You're hardly naive.'

It didn't take much imagination for it all to fall into place. 'Let me guess,' she began pensively. 'You came here purposely with your aunt, who conveniently happens to be a good friend of the del Santos, aware of their social standing and the opportunity to use them to include you in numerous invitations around the city. Thus ensuring regular social contact with Miguel.'

A tinkling laugh escaped Camille's lips. 'How clever of you, *chérie*. Naturally, the Australian visit was my suggestion.'

Hannah's eyes assumed a fiery sparkle. 'Do we draw battle lines?'

'As long as you understand Miguel is mine.' Camille's smile was entirely lacking in humour.

'Really?' Hannah posed with deliberate sarcasm. 'Aren't you forgetting I have an advantage or two?'

'Miguel might view you as an obligation,' the Frenchwoman relayed with pitiless asperity, 'but, darling, I intend to be his titillation.'

The peal of the telephone came as a welcome interruption, and Hannah crossed to take the call, aware as she did so that the Frenchwoman had turned towards the door. Within seconds she had departed, and Hannah gathered her wits together, answering a client's query, then, when she was done, she set to restoring order to the racks Camille had deliberately disorganised.

Tension knotted her stomach. It was worse, much worse than she'd envisaged. How would Miguel react if she told him? Be amused, probably. But what would lie beneath the humour? Male satisfaction? The thrill of the chase, the challenge? More pertinently, would he indulge in an extra-marital affair?

Dear God, she hoped not. Even the thought that he might almost destroyed her.

The peal of the telephone interrupted her reflection, and she took the call, attended to a client who bought a skirt, two blouses, a beautiful silk scarf, and on Cindy's return she collected her bag and crossed the street to lunch in a trendy café.

Hannah ordered a latte and a salad bagel, sipped the first and picked at the second, only to discard it entirely and order another latte.

Usually she took only sufficient time to eat before returning to the boutique, but today she chose to browse a few shops and view exquisite antique jewellery. A pair of earrings caught her eye, and she entered the shop, tried them on, then bought them in a moment of impulse.

It was almost two when she re-entered the boutique, four when Cindy left for the day, and at five-fifteen she locked up and drove home.

As hard as she tried, it was impossible to dismiss Camille from her mind. What she'd first thought was a transitory game had now proven to hold premeditated intent. Dealing with it could be akin to walking through a minefield.

One thing for sure...Miguel was *hers*. And she intended to fight for him, her marriage, her life, she determined as she garaged the car and made her way into the house.

Sofia was in the kitchen preparing dinner, and Hannah greeted her fondly as she crossed to the refrigerator.

'There are messages for you, and two for the *se-ñor*,' the housekeeper informed her as she wielded a chopping knife with considerable dexterity. 'I put them in the *señor*'s study.'

Hannah extracted a bottle of chilled water and poured some into a glass. 'Thanks. I'll go check them in a minute.' A piquant aroma teased her nostrils. 'Mmm,' she murmured appreciatively. 'Something smells delicious.'

'Seafood,' Sofia enlightened. 'Served with a mixed salad.'

She lifted the glass to her lips and took a long swallow, then moved to the cook-top and lifted the lid on the gently simmering saucepan. The temptation to retrieve a steaming mussel was too great, and she quickly passed the hot shell from one hand to the other as she tore it apart and extracted the succulent flesh.

'You want? I pull some out and put on a plate,' Sofia determined, and Hannah shook her head.

'No, I'll save it for dinner.' Her stomach growled in protest of insufficient sustenance. 'I'll go shower and change. Is Miguel home?'

'The *señor* ring an hour ago. Delayed. I serve dinner at seven. Okay?'

Hannah savoured the mussel flesh, and followed it with yet another glass of water. Maybe she'd go swim a few lengths in the pool first. She had time, and she felt strangely restless with a need to expend some nervous energy.

It took only minutes to reach her bedroom, and a

few more to discard her clothes and don an aqua bikini. Then she caught up a beach towel from the linen closet, quickly retraced her steps and made her way through the wide set of French doors at the rear of the house to the tiled pool area.

Heaven, she breathed a short while later as she cleaved sure strokes through the cool salt-chlorinated water.

She didn't allow herself to think, only focused on the silky feel of the water against her skin, the weightlessness of her body and the measured movement of her arms and legs.

It was so quiet, with no neighbourhood noise to disturb the air. High walls, with tall trees lining the boundaries, lent a secluded atmosphere, making it difficult to believe a large cosmopolitan city hummed with vibrant life mere kilometres away.

She could be anywhere, she mused, intent for a few seconds imagining a place far removed from here, where there were no phones, no social obligations, no distractions. Just her, with Miguel. Lazing in the sun, relaxing. Making love, eating when they felt the need for food, and sleeping when everything else palled.

Except that was a fantasy. Reality was a hurried break in between scheduled meetings...whether it was Paris, Rome, Madrid or Frankfurt. A snatched day here and there, always within reach of a mobile phone and an important call that inevitably broke the spell.

It was life in the fast lane. The need to make and close the next deal. To build and expand, to consolidate and venture into new fields. Always a step ahead of the competitors.

Like a merry-go-round that kept moving, once you were on it was hard to get off.

Maybe she could persuade Miguel to fit a holiday into his schedule. Hawaii. All that sun, surf and sand, where the pace was slower, and the outer islands offered a relaxed, carefree lifestyle.

Hannah didn't hear the faint splash as Miguel dived cleanly into the pool, and it was only when his head broke the surface close by that she became aware she was no longer alone.

She turned towards him and trod water as he reached her side. 'Hi. You're home early.'

Miguel paused to sweep water from his face and smooth both hands over his head, leaving his hair a sleek ebony. 'Impossible, of course, that I might want to be with my wife?'

Hannah tilted her head to one side and cast him a considering look. 'Hmm, maybe.'

'Gracias, amada,' he teased lightly. 'For the vote of confidence.' He moved close and cradled her hips, then eased both hands beneath the thin fabric to cup her bottom.

A delicious shiver feathered the length of her spine, and her body arched into his of its own accord, exulting in the touch of hair-roughened thighs against her smooth skin.

Her hands instinctively linked together at his nape, and she angled her mouth as his slanted to capture hers in a sensual tasting that began slowly, sweetly, then began to build into something that became an evocative preliminary to the promise of passion.

She wanted more, much more than this as the slide of his hands wreaked havoc in seeking sensitised pleasure pulses, and a faint groan sighed in her throat at the prospect of what he intended to do.

But not here. She possessed few inhibitions, but making love in the pool in daylight when there was every possibility Sofia might happen into view did much to kill her spontaneity.

Had they been completely alone... Slowly Hannah broke the kiss, and regretfully unwound her hands from his neck. 'Dinner will be ready soon, and we both need to shower and dress.'

Miguel let her go, his eyes dark with lambent emotion. 'I guess we could indulge in a leisurely shower.'

It was her turn to tease. 'Be late for dinner, and ruin Sofia's paella?'

He pressed a quick hard kiss to her parted lips.

'It will keep, *querida*.' And the promise, the erotic wait would present a slow torture...for both of them. Afterwards, she would weep for the release, and cry from the mutual joy of it.

She completed a few side-strokes and reached the tiled ledge, then she pulled herself over it to stand in one lithe movement, aware Miguel mirrored her actions.

In unison they each caught up a towel, removed the excess moisture, then hitched it securely and made their way indoors.

Halfway up the stairs Miguel hoisted her slender

frame over one shoulder and carried her the rest of the way.

'Caveman tactics?' Hannah queried to the broad expanse of his back, and felt rather than heard his faint rumble of laughter.

'You object?'

She clung onto his shoulders, felt the shift and play of powerful muscles as he moved towards the bedroom.

'Would it make any difference?'

Miguel entered their suite, closed the door, then lowered her down to stand in front of him. 'You don't want to play?'

Hannah looked at him carefully, saw the sensual curve of his mouth and glimpsed the darkness in his eyes.

'Yes,' she answered simply, and tried not to wish with all her heart that it was *her* he needed, not just the woman who bore his name.

He made lovemaking an art form, and she told herself she didn't care. It was enough he could make her feel like this. Enough that together they created a sexual magic that transmuted sheer sensation and became exquisite ecstasy.

Desire flared...wild, mesmeric and primitive as instinct met with hunger, and ravaged them both.

Afterwards they showered, then dressed in casual clothes before making their way downstairs, choosing to collect the delectable paella and eat on the patio adjoining the pool.

Occasionally they paused to tempt each other with

a forkful of food, and they sipped a fine white wine, ate crusty bread, and watched the summer sun slowly sink over the horizon.

They took time to discuss the day, and Hannah deliberately made no mention of Camille. Somehow it seemed almost a sacrilege to spoil the moment, and the night.

Outdoor lights provided a soft glow, illuminating the gardens, throwing long shadows from surrounding shrubbery. Moths fluttered around the electric lamps, fascinated by the brightness.

It was a while before they silently collected plates, glassware and cutlery and returned them to the kitchen.

'Tired?'

'A little,' she answered honestly as he mobilised the alarm system.

He held out his hand and she curled her fingers within his as they ascended the stairs. In the bedroom he removed her clothes, then his own, drawing her down onto the bed before gathering her close into the curve of his body.

She succumbed to sleep within minutes, and Miguel lay staring with brooding reflectiveness into the darkness, all too aware of the rhythmic beat of her heart beneath the palm of his hand, the faint muskiness of her feminine scent, the clean, fresh fragrance of her hair as her head nestled close in against the curve of his shoulder.

She moved, snuggling closer, and the hand that rested at the edge of his waist slipped down to his hip. She slept, for her breathing pattern remained un-changed.

He shifted his head slightly to brush his lips to the edge of her forehead and a faint smile softened his mouth as a soft sound sighed from her lips.

Independent, strong, individualistic, he mused as he courted sleep. A generous and passionate lover who matched him with an equal hunger of her own.

His.

CHAPTER FOUR

THE day began badly with a phone call from Cindy's mother to say Cindy had been rushed into hospital for an emergency appendectomy and wouldn't be able to return to work for at least a week.

Hannah felt genuinely upset, for Cindy was a friend as well as someone who worked part-time in the boutique, and she organised flowers to be sent to the hospital, made plans to visit after work, then began ringing the first of two women who made themselves available to work when required.

The first was overseas, the second had a family emergency, and her only recourse was an employment agency. Failing any success there, she could call on her mother, if only to fill in for an hour around midday.

Breakfast was a non-event, with only time to swallow half a glass of orange juice and follow it with a few sips of coffee.

'Por Dios,' Miguel swore swiftly as she caught up her bag and slid the strap over one shoulder. *'Sit.'*

He reached out, closed his hand over her arm, and forced her into a nearby chair. 'Eat.' He pushed a plate towards her, split a croissant and spread conserve onto each half.

She threw him a wry look. 'I can't. I'll be late.'

'So be late,' he suggested evenly. 'Five minutes is all it will take. You could easily be caught up in traffic that long.'

'I'm not a child, dammit.'

'You're wasting time,' Miguel said imperturbably.

She *was* hungry, and failing finding someone to fill in, or if Renee wasn't available, she'd have to temporarily close the boutique for the ten minutes it would take to go fetch a sandwich.

Stubborn single-mindedness forbade that she actually *sat*, but she did eat both pieces of the croissant and followed it down with the rest of the fine, hot, sweet coffee.

'Satisfied?'

He cast her a brooding glance. 'No.'

She gathered up her car keys. 'You, of course, rarely suffer emergencies that toss your schedule out the window.'

'Occasionally,' Miguel conceded.

'Don't tell me—you always have a back-up plan,' she responded drily.

'A few minutes ago you couldn't wait to leave,' he drawled, arching an eyebrow. 'Now you want to argue?'

'Why, when I never win?' Hannah flung with exasperation, and threw him a startled glance as he moved swiftly to cup her face.

He angled her mouth to meet his in an evocative kiss that tore at her emotions and made her wish she could take the time to deepen and savour it. Then she was free.

She could only look at him, her eyes wide and un-blinking. Just when she thought she could predict how he'd react, he managed to surprise her.

She unconsciously moistened her lips, aware her mouth shook slightly, and saw his eyes flare briefly.

'Go, *querida*. I'll call you through the day.' Hannah turned away from him and moved quickly through the foyer to the garage.

Could the day get any worse? she queried silently as she put a call through to her mother, only to discover Renee was *en route* to the airport to catch a scheduled flight to Sydney.

'I'll be back tonight, darling. Tomorrow is fine, if you need me. I'll ring when I get in.'

Within minutes of opening the boutique she rang the first of two agencies on her list, and felt immeasurably relieved to discover half an hour later they had a suitable salesgirl available to report for work the next day.

Hannah was kept busy all morning as several clients came by to examine the latest delivery of new stock. Telephoned requests to put some items aside for a few hours meant the boutique wasn't empty for long.

At midday she affixed a 'back in ten minutes' sign on the door, locked up and quickly crossed the street to a nearby café. A salad sandwich with coffee to take away would assuage her hunger, and with luck she might even get to eat it without any interruption.

'Hannah.'

The sultry accent caused the hairs to rise on the

back of her neck. *Tell me I'm wrong*, she pleaded silently, only to turn and discover Camille seated at a nearby table.

The Frenchwoman's presence *here* seemed too co-incidental. Another of Camille's ploys to draw atten-tion to her knowledge of Hannah's daily routine?

'Camille,' Hannah acknowledged with forced ci-vility as she stood waiting for her order to be filled.

'Why don't you join me?'

Not if I can help it. 'I have to get back. Perhaps some other time?' An empty suggestion she had no intention of fulfilling.

'I'll call in later.'

Hannah barely resisted the temptation to say *please don't* as the girl behind the counter handed over a capped take-away cup and a plastic container with her sandwich.

'Bye, Camille.' The words were merely a courtesy as she turned towards the door. She didn't want to play *friend* with the stunning Frenchwoman. If she had a choice, she'd prefer not to have anything to do with her at all! However, the chances of that were slim, given Camille's determination.

The phone was ringing when she unlocked the bou-tique and she hurried forward to answer it. Within minutes of replacing the receiver, it pealed again.

'I've been gifted tickets to a film premiere tonight,' Miguel began without preamble. He named the title and the venue. 'I'll be home at six.'

'*Gracias,*' Hannah declared, and his husky laughter was almost her undoing.

'Take care, *querida*. Don't work too hard.'

Fat chance, Hannah thought as she juggled attending to clients and phone calls in between snatching a bite to eat.

There was satisfaction in selecting beautifully crafted garments to suit a certain occasion for a favoured client. Offering suggestions for footwear, accessories, even jewellery, was something she viewed as an art form. The client's pleasure and continued loyalty was her reward. So much so that when she bought she did so with specific clients in mind.

It wasn't just a job. It never had been. Hannah doubted it ever would be. The prospect of selling the boutique, or retiring and letting a *vendeuse* manage it, hadn't occurred to her. Although there would probably come a time when she considered children. Having a child was an important issue in their marriage, given the main reason for the union was to legally ensure two united family fortunes continued into another generation.

However, *when* this should happen hadn't consciously been decided. Miguel had agreed to her suggestion they wait a year or two, and she had considered maybe thirty might be a good age to discard contraception.

Why was she suddenly given to thinking like this? Because Camille posed a threat?

Dammit, you didn't have a child to use as a bargaining tool, much less a weapon!

The electronic buzzer dispersed her train of

thought, and she endeavoured to keep her smile in place as she recognised Camille.

Talk of the devil!

'I enjoyed a long lunch, then spent an hour or two browsing the boutiques,' Camille informed her as she crossed to where several silk shirts were displayed.

'I caught sight of something here yesterday that I thought I should have.' She slid hangers every which way and a slight frown creased her brow. 'Perhaps you've put it aside?' She described the shirt, named the label, the size, then looked askance at Hannah as if she might conjure it up out of thin air.

'I sold it yesterday afternoon.'

'Order one in for me.'

It was a command, not a request, and Hannah held her breath for a few seconds before slowly releasing it. 'I can try,' she said evenly. 'However, everything here is limited edition stock.'

Camille gave her a long considering look. 'Make the call. I want it.'

Hannah viewed her carefully, then threw politeness out the window. 'You can't always have what you want.'

There was no mistaking her meaning.

The Frenchwoman examined her perfectly manicured nails, then seared Hannah with a vindictive glare.

'You're wrong, *chérie*. I *always* get what I want.'

'Really?' Her cynicism was marked. 'Maybe it's time you didn't.'

Camille resembled a hissing cat about to strike. 'So you intend to fight?'

This could rapidly digress into something feral. 'I won't gift-wrap Miguel and hand him to you on a platter.'

'Why, *chérie*. I don't need for you to gift me anything. I reach out and take what I want.'

She could feel her fingers curling in against each palm, and it was all she could do to stay calm. 'Even if it doesn't belong to you?'

'The fact it doesn't belong to me merely adds to the attraction. Marriage? What is it?' Camille emphasised the point with a Gallic shrug. 'Merely a piece of paper.'

'Try sacred vows citing fidelity, trust and honour,' Hannah cited, and heard the Frenchwoman's pitying laughter.

'Poor *enfant*,' Camille chided. 'So naive and caught up with ideals.'

Ideals, huh? She was as well versed in reality as the next person. More so, because she'd grown up very aware there were those who would adopt any façade if they thought it would work to their advantage. Luc was the only one who'd managed to pull the wool over her eyes.

'What if Miguel won't play your game?' Hannah queried deliberately.

Camille broke into disbelieving laughter and shot her a pitying look. 'That is not an option.'

'You're so *sure* of yourself?'

'Sure of my—' she paused fractionally '—ability, darling.'

'Singular?' Hannah posed with wry cynicism, determined not to concede this verbal match in any way.

'Perhaps we should agree to confer a week from now. You might not be so confident.' With that parting shot, Camille swept out of the boutique and soon disappeared from sight.

Phew! She might not have won that round, but she hadn't exactly lost.

It was after five when she left the boutique, and she drove to the hospital, visited a slightly wan Cindy, then headed home.

Miguel had showered and was in the process of dressing when Hannah entered the bedroom.

His taut, steel-muscled body projected an enviable aura of power. A strength that was also of the mind and spirit, and she would have given anything to be able to go to him, have him enfold her close, and make the world go away.

Well, maybe the *world* was asking too much. All she wanted was for Camille Dalfour to be gone.

'Bad day?'

She lifted her head and threw him a wry look as she shrugged out of her jacket and began unbuttoning her blouse. 'Tomorrow has to be better.'

He reached for his shirt and pulled it on. 'Want to cancel out tonight?'

What she wanted was to relax in the spa-bath for as long as it took for her tense muscles to unknot, then indulge in a long, sweet loving.

'No. The movie received good reviews overseas,' she said evenly.

Miguel's hands stilled at the faint catch in her voice, and he cast her a discerning look, saw the soft shadows beneath her eyes, cheeks that were devoid of colour, and he covered the distance between them in a few easy steps.

He cupped her chin, lifting it so she had no recourse but to meet his gaze. 'Something bothers you?'

Yes, it bothers me like hell. 'As I said,' she prevaricated as both of his thumbs smoothed a soothing pattern along the edge of her jaw, 'a bad day.'

'Hannah.' His voice was a silky drawl. 'Don't take me for a fool. Honesty, remember?'

Well, this was it. There wasn't going to be a better time. 'Camille wants you.'

His eyes darkened, although his expression didn't change. 'She has told you this?' The query held an icy softness. 'When?'

She held his gaze without difficulty. 'Yesterday, and today.' She attempted a smile, and failed miserably. 'You're a marked man.'

'Indeed?' His voice was a cynical drawl.

This time the smile was bright, too bright. 'She's convincing.'

'I'm sure she is.'

'I assured her I possess a few advantages.' She lifted a hand and began counting off her fingers. 'Minor things like a hefty inheritance, a convenient and compatible marriage. *You.*' She cast him a measured look. 'Did I get those in the right order?'

His eyes darkened and became obsidian shards. 'I could shake you.'

'Please don't,' she protested slowly. 'I might shatter.'

Nevertheless he did, gently. 'You sweet fool,' he growled in husky chastisement. 'I am not interested in extra-marital games.' He traced her lower lip with the pad of his thumb, then released her. '*Comprende?*'

'Words, Miguel?' she queried with a hint of sadness. 'Don't insult me by uttering them meaninglessly.'

'Why would I risk our marriage?'

'Exactly.' Something inside her died at the way he obviously regarded their alliance. 'Why would you?'

'Hannah.' The silky warning was evident, but she chose to ignore it.

'To Camille, you're a challenge.'

'Women of Camille's ilk,' Miguel evinced hardly, 'are known to have their own agenda.'

Hannah's eyes sparked with blue fire. 'Well, she can take her agenda and go shove it.'

Amusement lifted the corners of his mouth, and his eyes assumed a humorous gleam. 'At daggers drawn, *querida?*'

'Yes.'

His gaze narrowed slightly. 'You're not in her league.'

'I hope that's a compliment?'

'Without doubt.' He leant down and brushed his lips to her temple. 'Go have your shower.'

Hannah caught up fresh underwear, a wrap, and entered the *en suite*, emerging fifteen minutes later to discover Miguel had already gone downstairs.

She pulled on smart jeans and a rib-knit top, twisted her hair into a knot on top of her head, then she joined Miguel in the dining room.

Sofia had excelled herself with the meal, and an accompanying light white wine provided a relaxing effect.

It took only minutes to clear the table and stack the dishwasher before returning upstairs to change.

Hannah selected an evening trouser suit in brilliant sapphire, brushed her hair loose, and tended to her make-up before adding a knee-length sheer silk evening jacket patterned in green and blue peacock hues. A beaded evening purse completed the outfit.

'*Exquisita*,' Miguel complimented, and she gave him an impish smile.

'*Gracias, hombre*.' She cast his tall frame a considering look, deliberately noting the splendid dark evening suit, the snowy white cotton shirt, the neat black bow tie. 'Not bad.' A mischievous smile curved her generous mouth. 'I guess you'll do.'

'Indeed?' He took in her finely boned features, the petite stature that never failed to stir in him a host of emotions. 'Shall we leave?'

They arrived fifteen minutes before the premiere was due to begin, and walked into the crowded foyer as invited patrons were entering the auditorium.

The film had an unusual premise, one that enchanted the mind, yet held an underlying thread which provided a startling conclusion. The acting was superb, and it was touted that the three main actors would receive Academy Award nominations.

Miguel reached for her hand as the credits rolled, and together they slipped from the darkened theatre ahead of the general exodus.

'Feel like going somewhere for coffee?'

Hannah almost declined, then changed her mind. 'Why not?'

They walked a block, then entered an arcade whose decor was late nineteenth century, and chose a small café specialising in imported coffee and delicate home-made savouries and cakes.

No one seemed to be in a hurry, and it was an ideal niche to relax, unwind, and just *be*.

They both ordered liqueur coffees, and selected a small delicacy to sample.

'My cousin Alejandro and his wife Elise are flying in for the weekend,' Miguel told her as he sweetened his coffee. 'They'll attend the Leukaemia Foundation charity ball as our guests on Saturday evening.'

Hannah offered him a warm smile. She'd only met Elise a few times since the wedding, but they shared a friendly empathy. 'How long are they staying?'

'Only a few days. Elise is leaving the two boys with a nanny and flying north to spend time with friends while Alejandro is in Perth.'

'You're going with him.' It was a statement, not a query, and Miguel glimpsed the fleeting emotions evident in her expressive features.

'You could join me.'

Hannah almost said *yes*. Then she remembered Cindy was unavailable, and leaving the boutique in a stranger's hands wasn't an option. 'I'd love to,' she said regretfully. 'But I can't.' She gave a resigned shrug. 'How long will you be away?'

'Two, maybe three days.'

Two lonely nights. She could go visit her parents, connect with a few friends and organise a night at the theatre, take in a movie, maybe go out to dinner. Numerous possibilities to occupy her time. Except she'd miss him like crazy.

Did he possess an inkling how much he meant to her? Somehow she doubted it. Fondness and affection didn't equate to *love*. And duty was an empty substitute.

'The boutique—'

'Is important to you.'

She looked at him carefully, silently imploring him to understand. 'We agreed—'

'I know.'

'It's the one thing I've done totally on my own,' she said simply.

'I'm not questioning your ability to achieve success in your own right.'

'No. But you want me to choose.'

'The social circuit in favour of the boutique?' He arched a quizzical eyebrow. 'Not your style, Hannah.'

'What are you suggesting?'

'Give Cindy a promotion. Elevate her to manageress, cultivate two relieving saleswomen who can work in your place.'

'Thus leaving me available to travel with you at short notice?'

'I would prefer to have you with me, than leave you at home.'

A concession? An admission of sorts? 'I'll give it serious thought,' she conceded, and saw his gleaming smile.

'Do that, *amada*.' He drained what remained of his coffee. 'Shall we leave?'

It was late when Miguel garaged the car, and on entering their bedroom Hannah removed her clothes, her make-up, and slid between the cool percale sheets.

She fell asleep within minutes, drifting effortlessly into oblivion where scattered dreams invaded her subconscious mind until the early hours, when the light brush of fingers trailing the indentations of her spine brought her slowly into a state of lazy wakefulness.

Hannah arched her body in a feline stretch, then turned towards the man who was bent on creating havoc with her senses.

With deliberate playfulness she traced a teasing pattern over the dark whorls of hair that smattered his chest, dipping the tips of her nails and gently dragging them across his pectoral muscles before trailing to his navel.

She heard his faint intake of breath, and explored lower, barely touching the engorged tumescent shaft as she sought the apex between his thighs.

In one fluid movement she rose into a sitting position and swept aside the bedcovers, aware of his hands as they caressed her breasts, bringing the dusky peaks into tingling arousal.

Her hair was loose, its length tousled from sleep, and she bent her head so that it brushed against the most sensitised part of his body in a movement that brought him to the brink.

With a soft growl he closed his hands over her waist as he deftly swung her round to sit astride him, and she gasped out loud as his fingers touched her intimately.

Sensation arrowed through her body as he gently rocked her back and forth, until it was she who cried out his name and begged for his possession.

He gave it, lifting her so that she slowly took him deep inside as her body lowered onto him, and then it was she who held the power, she who set the pace, until he removed it from her and took over.

Together they sought the pinnacle and soared the heights in perfect accord. A slow, beautiful sharing of the ultimate meshing of mind, body and soul.

Such attuned sensuality robbed her of the ability to speak, even to move for what seemed an age, then she gently subsided against his chest, nuzzling her lips into the curve of his neck.

His hands brushed the length of her back, caressed her buttocks, returned to slide through the length of her hair as he angled her head towards his, seeking her mouth in a kiss that made her want to weep with its gentle evocativeness.

He traced a path over every inch of her skin, lingering over pleasure pulses, teasing them into vibrant life until she pleaded for him to stop.

'Are you sure you want me to?' Miguel teased in a soft accented drawl, and he gave a low husky laugh at her denial.

What followed was a tantalisingly slow loving as he followed the trail of his hand with his mouth, using it as an erotic instrument that made her totally *his*. Passion flared as he surged into her, raw and primitive, an exotic hunger that was libidinous and almost beyond control.

Afterwards they slept a little, exhausted, until dawn filtered silvered fingers of light through the diminishing darkness, slowly painting soft muted colour over land and sea until the emerging sun feathered a faint golden glow, giving substance to shadows as it heralded a new day.

Hannah woke to an awareness of weightlessness and the knowledge she was being carried. There was also the faint hum of tumbling water, and the slight scent of aromatic oils.

Within seconds Miguel lowered her into the pulsing spa-bath, then stepped in to sit opposite.

He looked far too vibrant for her peace of mind, and she scooped up a handful of water and aimed it at him, watching his gleaming smile as he returned the favour.

With automatic movements she twisted the length of her hair atop her head and secured it with a pin from a nearby shell-shaped dish.

It was a perfect way to begin the day. All of it.

The lovemaking, which she refused at this moment to call *sex*, the sheer bliss of curling into her lover's arms, and now the shared luxury of gently pulsing jets to ease away the slight pull of overused muscles.

She wanted to lean her head back, close her eyes, and stay here for hours. Perhaps enjoy a champagne breakfast, with fresh strawberries followed by eggs Benedict, crispy bacon and two cups of strong black sweet coffee. Then crawl back to bed and sleep beneath the covers until the sun rose to its zenith.

Sadly, it was the wrong day. The weekend didn't begin until tomorrow, and the boutique awaited, as did the replacement saleswoman. And then there was *Camille*.

Slowly she opened her eyes.

'Where did you go?' Miguel queried gently, and she smiled at him.

'You don't want to know.'

'If you tell me, I can—'

'Wave your magic wand?'

'Make a few calls, pull a string or two.'

'Ah, I believe you would. But it's not that simple. Besides, this one's mine, *querido*.' She reached out a hand and snagged a towel, then stepped out from the spa-bath.

It wasn't nearly as late as she'd thought, she discovered as she dressed in the exquisitely tailored gear she chose to wear to work.

There was time for a leisurely breakfast before catching hold of her briefcase and following Miguel through to the garage.

The automatic door lifted, and almost in unison they unlocked each vehicle, slid in behind the wheels, engaged the ignitions, and at Miguel's signal Hannah reversed out ahead of him.

At the end of the street, she lifted a hand and waved, glancing in her rear-vision mirror as she turned in the opposite direction.

The replacement salesgirl arrived late, and, although her credentials appeared satisfactory, she was more suited to the teen section in a department store than catering to a very particular clientele demanding exclusive and expensive designer labels.

Hannah did her best to provide a crash course in haute couture, but after one disastrous clash with a client she relegated Chantal to menial tasks, and had her fetch lunch.

By mid-afternoon Hannah had a tension headache, Chantal had called it quits, which meant another call to the agency, impressing very specific needs, and a desperate call to Renee who willingly agreed to fill in for a few hours the next day.

There was a brief moment when Hannah seriously considered Miguel's suggestion to promote Cindy. But first, she decided a trifle grimly, she had to get through the next week or two.

CHAPTER FIVE

THE gown Hannah chose to wear for the evening's soirée was a full-length slim-fitting creation in ice-blue silk with a halter-neck and flaring into soft folds from the knee. A soft cowl effect provided an attractive *décolletage*. Matching blue stiletto-heeled shoes and a gem-encrusted evening purse completed the outfit.

Jewellery was confined to a diamond tear-drop necklace suspended on a slim gold chain, with earrings to match, and a diamond tennis bracelet at her wrist.

Make-up was kept to a minimum, with emphasis on her eyes, a light rose colouring her lips, and she swept her hair into a sleek chignon.

The prestigious charity event owed its success to an active and imaginative committee, a guest-list of the city's social élite, a luxurious venue, fine food and wine, and top-line entertainment.

This particular end-of-year function numbered as the jewel in the crown of charity events, with the funds raised being donated to the Leukaemia Foundation.

Miguel looked resplendent in a formal black dinner suit, white shirt and black bow-tie. Superb tailoring accentuated his breadth of shoulder and tall muscular

Their respective fathers were brothers who had each left the land of their birth to seek a fortune in another country, succeeded, married and produced one son.

Alejandro resided in Sydney, with his wife Elise and two young children. The Santanas name was well respected in the business arena, and both Alejandro and Miguel shared a mutual stake in a few financial ventures.

Hannah embraced Elise warmly. 'It's so good to see you. When did you arrive?'

'Midday. Alejandro has only used the cell-phone once, and has yet to open the laptop.' She gave an irrepressible smile. 'And I've only checked with the nanny twice.'

Hannah's eyes twinkled with humour. 'This is the first time you've left them at home?'

'Second,' Elise owned. 'It doesn't get any easier.'

'She has a compulsive need to check on the children's welfare,' Alejandro drawled as he leant forward to brush a kiss to Hannah's cheek.

'Of course,' Elise acceded, sending her husband a long glance of the kind that made Hannah's nerves shimmer with envy.

'We're seated together,' Hannah indicated, and watched as Elise slid into a chair, then patted the one next to her.

'Sit beside me. We have so much to catch up on.'

There was background music, and the majority of guests were already seated.

There were only two empty seats at their table, and

frame. He presented a forceful image that
a dramatic mesh of latent sensuality and e
ruthlessness. Add an enviable aura of power,
effect was lethal.

'Ready?'

Hannah offered him a sparkling smile. 'To g
battle?'

His husky chuckle caused a shivery sensation
slither down her spine.

'Is that how you see tonight's social event?'

She wrinkled her nose, and resorted to humour.

'It'll be a dazzling occasion, with the usual play
ers.'

Including Camille, she added silently, offering a
fervent prayer the society princess wasn't included in
the guests seated at their particular table.

The Deity wasn't listening, she determined an hour
later as she slid into reserved seating and saw
Camille's name on a place-card next to Miguel.

Damn. Could she surreptitiously switch it? Suiting
thought to deed, she quickly transposed the place-card
with that of a guest seated opposite.

Alejandro and Elise were a welcome inclusion, and
anyone seeing Miguel and Alejandro together could
not fail to note they shared relatives in common. They
were of a similar height and possessed the same
breadth of shoulder, the same physically fit stature
and ease of movement. Even their facial features bore
a certain similarity, the sculpted angles and planes,
piercing dark eyes, that beautifully moulded sensual
mouth.

Hannah had to concede Camille made a stunning entrance, clothed in a deep red creation that covered her perfect body like a second skin.

Hannah's gaze slid to Camille's partner, and froze in shocked disbelief for all of three seconds before she quickly masked her expression.

Luc Dubois.

Dear heaven. It was three years since she'd last seen him.

Then, he'd been a charming rake whose main occupation was insinuating himself into the lives of wealthy women. Young, not so young, it hadn't seemed to bother him. A photographic professional who used his skill to gain entry into the realm of the rich and famous.

She should know. For three months in Paris he'd exercised his considerable charms on *her*. Wined, dined, and eventually swept her off her feet and into his arms.

Now, Hannah watched as Camille began weaving her way towards them with Luc in tow, and she forced herself to maintain a polite smile as they drew close.

Had Miguel noted their entrance? Recognised Luc?

Apprehension scudded down her spine at the thought of his reaction when he did.

Although it was possible, she wasn't sure the two men had ever met. A hysterical bubble of laughter rose and died in her throat.

Dear heaven. Camille *and* Luc seated at their table? How cruel could fate be?

Hannah was aware the instant Miguel caught sight

of them, and could only wonder if anyone else noticed the way his body uncoiled and then became frighteningly still. Like a jungle animal scenting an enemy and assessing when to strike.

'Miguel, Hannah.' Camille resembled an aristocratic cat who'd just snacked on caviare and cream.

All it took was one glance at Camille's bland expression to guess that Luc's invitation had been deliberately orchestrated.

'Camille.' She thought her face would crack with the strain of keeping a smile pinned on her face as she acknowledged the Frenchwoman.

What was Luc doing here? Not so much Australia, or even Melbourne, but *this* particular charity event, *and* partnering Camille?

It didn't take a genius to arrive at the correct answer, Hannah decided wryly. Even the most kindly disposed person would suspect Camille of mischief-making. Luc's appearance *here* simply reinforced Hannah's belief that Camille was not only serious in her pursuit of Miguel, but she'd stop at nothing to gain her objective.

So it was *war*. Well, she was very good at self-protection. She had years of experience in dealing with it. If Camille thought snaring Miguel would be a walkover, she had another think coming!

'You know each other, of course,' Camille purred as she slid into her seat, and Hannah opted for confrontational strategy.

'The media made much of it at the time.' She

looked at Luc, wanting to sear him to a burnt frizzle on the spot. 'I hope they paid you well.'

'Handsomely.' His smile would have melted many a hardened female heart.

But not hers. 'Let me introduce my husband, Miguel Santanas.'

Miguel was incredibly polite. Anyone who knew him would have blanched at the icy silkiness apparent in his voice.

Luc, however, seemed totally oblivious.

Wine stewards began serving drinks, and the event began with an introductory speech by the charity chairwoman, followed by the MC who outlined the evening's entertainment.

The organisation was very smooth as models strutted the catwalk to funky music while waiters served the starter.

Hannah looked at the artistically arranged seafood in a bed of salad greens, and merely forked a few morsels, her appetite seriously impaired by the presence of not one enemy, but *two*, in her immediate vicinity.

She would have given anything to be able to walk out of the ballroom and take a taxi home. Except that would amount to running away, and her pride forbade such an option.

Pretend, a tiny voice urged, and act as if you don't have a care in the world.

Miguel ordered champagne, and indicated that the steward should fill her flute. Hannah cast him an enquiring glance and caught the faint smile curving the edge of his mouth, the steady gleam apparent as he raised his glass in a silent salute.

He knew, of course, exactly who Luc Dubois was, and the part Luc had played in her life.

'What is this in aid of?' Hannah queried quietly, slanting one eyebrow in quizzical humour as she touched the rim of her flute to his. 'Courage?'

'Do you need it?'

She inclined her head slightly, and offered with soft-edged mockery, 'This is going to be one hell of an evening.'

'Do you want to leave?'

Her eyes widened. He'd do that for her? 'No.' Her voice was steady, but inside her heart missed a beat.

The models concluded showing the after-five segment, and the MC announced a well-known comedian who delivered a few amusing and occasionally risqué anecdotes while an army of waiters removed plates and the stewards tended to the guests' drinking needs.

Two singers performed two numbers, after which the models returned to the catwalk with a comprehensive display of evening wear.

It was while the main course was being served that Camille chose to engage Miguel's attention with a flirtatious coquetry that made Hannah barely refrain from grinding her teeth in angry vexation.

'Am I missing something here?' Elise ventured, *sotto voce*. 'Or is the beautiful Camille on a flirting mission with Miguel?'

'If he responds,' Hannah murmured, 'he's dead meat.'

'Luc is the smokescreen, or the ammunition?'

'Both, I imagine.'

Elise's features softened in empathy. 'Tread carefully.'

Now would be a good time to utilise the powder room, and with a murmured excuse she slipped out from her chair.

Miguel could indulge in polite conversation with Camille if he chose, but *she* didn't have to stay and watch Camille's play-acting!

'I'll come with you.' Elise rose to her feet and together they began making their way towards one of the exits.

Hannah paused to greet a few friends as she threaded her way through the ballroom, and she took unnecessary time freshening her make-up.

Elise joined her after using the facilities, and she pressed a hand to her waist, then groaned and vanished into a stall, only to emerge looking slightly pale and wan.

Comprehension was immediate. 'You're pregnant?'

Elise managed a faint smile. 'After two sons, *this* one has to be a girl. Already she's exerting her personality in a way neither of the two boys did.'

'Uh-huh,' Hannah conceded with an impish grin. 'I gather Alejandro knows?'

'He finds it incredibly amusing.'

'Naturally, he'll be captivated from the instant she's born and be hers to command within minutes.'

Elise's gaze misted. 'He's a wonderful father.'

'Are you okay?'

'Oh, yes. I get to throw up on a regular basis half-way through breakfast and dinner.' She opened her evening purse and produced a toothbrush and paste. 'Before and after, I'm fine.'

Minutes later, their make-up restored, they moved towards the door, only to see Alejandro standing immediately outside in the vestibule.

Oh, my, Hannah breathed silently. Elise was his most precious possession. It was evident in the way he looked at her, the protective arm that immediately circled her waist. Body language that was intense and evocative.

It must be wonderful to share that kind of emotion, to be twin halves of a whole, and so complete. Together they returned to their table, and Miguel cast her a discerning look as she regained her seat. She was willing to swear she caught a glimmer of amusement evident as she reached for her wine.

'Your meal has cooled.' He beckoned a waiter and instructed another plate be served. Something that was done with alacrity.

'I'm not really hungry.'

'Nevertheless you will eat something,' Miguel chastised silkily, and saw her eyes widen as he lifted a hand and brushed the edge of her cheek with his fingers.

'What are you doing?'

His mouth formed a sensual curve. 'It's called re-assurance.'

'The attentive husband bit, huh?' Hannah queried with a touch of mockery.

'Something like that.'

'For Camille's benefit?'

'Yours.'

Oh, he was good. Very, very good. She doubted anyone present observing their byplay could be in doubt as to his feelings. She could almost hear the unspoken comments...*fifteen months into the marriage, and look at them.*

She offered him a brilliant smile. 'Careful, *querido*, you're in danger of reaching overkill.'

He touched a thumb-pad to her lips. 'Think so?'

The lights dimmed, a spotlight hit the MC, and the charity organiser announced the amount of money raised for the night's function, alerted guests to the next gala evening, and indicated a return of the comedian.

Somehow Camille had managed to manoeuvre the seating so she occupied a chair next to Miguel, and Hannah had to commend her determination while silently condemning her to hell.

Hannah picked at the decorative fare on her plate, forked a few mouthfuls, then pushed the plate aside.

Camille took every opportunity to engage Miguel's attention with a light trail of red-lacquered nails on his sleeve, a touch to his hand, and her smile was a work of art in the seduction stakes.

The models took the catwalk for the final round while dessert was being served, and afterwards the waiters brought coffee while the singing duo closed the entertainment for the evening.

A DJ switched on special lighting effects, set the first of several CDs playing, and background music and recorded vocals encouraged those inclined to dance to take to the floor.

Now was the time for guests to mingle, table-hop and socialise with friends who were also present.

Alejandro and Elise communicated their intention to leave. 'Tomorrow,' Elise promised quietly. 'We'll catch up. I have photos, and the men have organised a day cruise and a picnic lunch.'

As they left a colleague crossed to their table to talk to Miguel, Camille slipped through the crowd heading for the ballroom exit, Miguel excused himself briefly and moved a few steps away as a friend joined the colleague, and within seconds Hannah was aware of someone taking Miguel's seat.

'How are you, Hannah?'

The male voice was familiar, and she turned slowly to face the man to whom it belonged.

'Luc,' she acknowledged coolly. 'Believe me, there is no need to observe the social niceties. I have nothing to say to you.'

'So cool,' Luc mocked. 'Still the ice princess, I see.'

'You expect me to believe your presence here is purely coincidental?'

He inclined his head in a gesture of musing cynicism. 'We could enjoy a conversation. Three years, Hannah. We have some catching up to do.'

'No,' she denied. 'We don't.'

'Why, *chérie*?' His smile aimed to melt her heart. 'It was good while it lasted.'

She could feel the anger begin to burn deep inside. 'Strange,' she remarked coolly. 'Our memories don't match.'

She fixed him with an icy glare. 'So let's cut the pretence, shall we?'

He spread his hands in an expressive gesture. 'Who's pretending? I was very fond of you.'

'Words,' Hannah dismissed. 'Suppose you tell me exactly why you're here?'

'This event?'

'Oh, for heaven's sake. Cut the game-playing. You know very well what I mean.'

'Are you ready for the facts, *chérie*?'

As ready as I'll ever be! She didn't bother answering, just sent him a fulminating look that spoke volumes.

He gave a voluble sigh. 'It will cost you.'

'No, it won't,' Hannah denied heartlessly. 'You owe me. For living the good life at the expense of my foolish generosity.'

He proffered a mocking smile. 'When did you become so cynical?'

'Three years ago.'

'All right, *chérie*. This one is on me, for old times' sake.'

'*Merci*,' she acknowledged in a voice as cold as an arctic ice floe.

'Camille sought me out, paid my air fare, and is

footing my accommodation,' he revealed, and she arched one eyebrow.

'And you're bent on playing both ends against the middle?'

He gave a negligent shrug. 'Your words, not mine.'

Hannah looked at him carefully, saw the handsome features, the rakish gleam evident in his expression, and wondered how on earth she could have been swayed by his charm. His megawatt smile had no effect whatsoever.

'Go get a life, Luc.'

'A word of warning, sweetheart,' he offered quietly. 'Camille is on a mission.'

'As if I didn't know?'

'Dance with me, and I could be persuaded to tell you more.'

He was unbelievable! 'Not even if my life depended on it!'

One eyebrow lifted in cynical amusement. 'Perhaps you're right.' He cast a glance in Miguel's direction.

'Miguel Santanas doesn't look the type of man who would willingly share.'

No, Hannah agreed, suppressing a slight shiver. Miguel's ownership was total.

'Maybe we could share a coffee somewhere and talk about old times.'

'You can't be serious?' He had such a thick skin, it was almost laughable. 'Yes, you are,' she acknowledged with a shake of her head.

'No hard feelings?'

She faced him squarely, her eyes steady. 'When

you report to Camille, tell her she doesn't stand a snowflake's chance in hell.' She stood to her feet, needing a change of scene, if only for a few minutes.

She turned from the table and saw Miguel's tall frame a few feet distant. He looked totally relaxed, his strong masculine features portraying interest as he listened to whatever his colleague had to say.

One glance at the expression in his eyes was sufficient for Hannah to realise he hadn't missed a thing. There was a darkness evident, a latent anger that was almost frightening.

She moved towards him, pausing as she reached his side while he performed an introduction, and she stood perfectly still as he reached for her hand and linked his fingers through her own.

Support? Protection? she wondered. Or was he merely staking a claim, making a statement?

The colleague excused himself and returned to a nearby table.

'Shall we leave?' Miguel queried with a faintly inflected drawl.

Hannah offered him a stunning smile, then lifted a hand and traced a light path along the edge of his jaw.

'And spoil Camille's fun?'

He caught her fingers and pressed an open-mouthed kiss to her palm, observing the way her eyes darkened in dilation. Her lips trembled slightly, and for one infinitesimal second she looked acutely vulnerable.

'You resemble a piece of fragile glass on the point of shattering,' Miguel said gently. 'Home, I think.'

Her chin tilted fractionally. 'I'm really very resilient.' She summoned a smile. 'Besides, there's music, and we should dance.'

They did, for a while, moving to the funky beat, then when it changed to something slower Miguel pulled her into his arms and held her close.

It was heaven. She could almost forget where they were, the time, the place, everything except the man and the emotions he was able to arouse.

She felt his lips brush the top of her head, then linger at her temple, and she made a sound in her throat as they settled just beneath one earlobe.

They fitted together so well, and this close she could feel his powerful thigh muscles, the strength of his arousal.

'I think we should go home.'

His soft laughter feathered sensation over the surface of her skin, and heat unfurled within, warming her body to fever pitch.

'Do you need to return to the table?'

She shook her head, and together they made their way towards the ballroom exit, pausing from time to time to speak to acquaintances. They were about to pass through the large double doors when they came face to face with Camille.

'You're not leaving?'

Hannah offered a polite smile. 'We both have an early start tomorrow.'

'Tired, darling?' Her expression was deliberately bland. 'Miguel must find your lack of stamina a little—' she paused slightly '—tiresome.'

'Perhaps *tired* is just a polite euphemism,' Hannah ventured sweetly, and almost held her breath at the sheer venom evident in Camille's gaze before it was quickly masked. 'Goodnight, Camille.'

There was little the striking brunette could do other than make a graceful retreat. However there was the promise—no, *threat*, Hannah amended as she walked at Miguel's side to the lift, that this was only the beginning of Camille's campaign.

She sat in silence as Miguel eased the car through the city streets, lost in contemplative thought.

Media speculation had run rife at the time of her engagement to Miguel, and the caption above their wedding photos had given allusion to it being an arranged union. Something that aroused public conjecture, and added fuel to the social gossip columns.

However, more than a year down the track, the conjecture had lessened, they'd settled easily into the pattern of marriage, work and social commitments.

'You're quiet.'

Hannah glanced at Miguel and could determine little from his expression in the car's dim interior.

'How perceptive,' she afforded wryly, and incurred his brief glance.

'Camille bothers you?'

'Clever, too.'

He waited a beat. 'And Luc?'

She didn't even have to think. 'Is ancient history.'

'Not from where I was standing.'

Hannah took a deep breath, then released it slowly. 'You should have stood closer.' She bit back a humourless laugh. 'Then you would have heard me tell him to go get a life and stay out of mine.'

'That was the extent of your conversation?' They reached Toorak and turned into a select residential avenue.

'Oh, there's just one other detail,' she revealed as he took another turn and slowed before the impressive set of gates guarding the entrance to their home. 'He revealed Camille has *you* firmly in her sights, and she'll go to any lengths to get you.' She watched as Miguel activated the remote, opening the gates, and the car eased forward onto the wide sweeping drive. The garage doors slid up automatically at the touch of another remote, then closed seconds later when he cut the engine.

Hannah slid out and walked to the door leading into the house, waited while Miguel tended to the lock, then she moved through to the foyer.

'Indeed?' he drawled with ill-disguised mockery. He paused at the foot of the beautiful staircase and subjected her to a searching appraisal. 'Is his role that of accomplice in Camille's diabolical scheme?'

'Yes.'

'Be careful, *querida*,' he warned silkily. 'He hurt you once. I won't tolerate him hurting you again.'

'*You* won't tolerate it?' She strove to conquer a complex mix of emotions. 'There's no need to play the jealous husband!'

'I prefer...protective.'

He didn't move, but she had the impression his

body tensed, and apprehension slithered over the surface of her skin.

'Luc—'

'Occupied a small part of your life before you committed to me,' Miguel drawled in a dangerously quiet voice.

Just as several women undoubtedly occupied his. A hollow feeling settled low in her stomach and radiated towards her heart. Dear heaven, just thinking about who they were and how many there might have been made her feel ill.

Hannah held his gaze for several long seconds, then she brushed past him and moved quickly up the stairs.

A hollow feeling settled round her heart as she traversed the gallery to their room, and inside she began removing her ear-studs, then she reached for the catch on her necklace.

Miguel entered the room and shrugged off his dinner jacket, loosened his shoes, and discarded his socks. The bow-tie came next, then he undid and removed his shirt.

Dammit, what was the matter with the catch? She cursed it beneath her breath, and followed it with another as Miguel crossed to her side.

'Stand still.'

She was incredibly aware of him, the raw primitive aura combined with the subtle scent of his skin and the sensual warmth of his body. There was a part of her that wanted to sink in against him and lift her face for his kiss, while another part wanted to pummel his chest with her fists.

Didn't he know how vulnerable she felt? How much of a threat she knew Camille to be? As to Luc…she wouldn't trust him as far as she could throw him.

Miguel freed the catch in a second, and he dropped the chain into her hand before placing a thumb and forefinger on her chin, lifting it so she had no choice but to look at him.

'*Por Dios.*' His eyes darkened, and a muscle bunched at the edge of his jaw. 'You think I cannot see what Camille is?' He traced a thumb along her jaw, then slid a hand to capture her nape. 'Credit me with some intelligence, *mi mujer.*'

'It's your libido she's aiming at,' Hannah returned succinctly. 'Not your intelligence.'

'You imagine I would slip easily into another woman's bed?' Miguel queried with chilling softness.

All she could do was look at him, her mind filled with haunting images that drove her almost to the brink of sanity.

'We promised each other fidelity,' she managed quietly.

'You have no reason to doubt my word.'

'Nor mine.'

His gaze seared hers, seeing beyond the surface, aware of her vulnerability, its cause, and he silently damned Camille for deliberately setting out to undermine it.

He moved his fingers to the zip fastening on her gown, releasing it slowly, then he slipped each shoulder strap free so the beaded silk slithered to a heap at her feet. All she wore beneath it was a pair of lacy satin briefs, and his hands skimmed to her waist, settled, then slid up to shape her breasts.

He slanted his head down to hers and took her mouth in a slow, drugging kiss that was wholly sensual, tasting, exploring, teasing, until she wound her arms round his neck and kissed him back.

She loved the feel of him, the glide of her fingers as she traced strong muscle and sinew. The silk-smooth skin, the powerful breadth of shoulder, the hard ribcage, his taut midriff.

He was wearing too many clothes, and she reached for his belt buckle, undid it, then set about freeing his trousers.

Hannah felt the need pulse through her body, heating her senses to fever pitch.

Now, dammit. *Now*. Hard and fast, and wild. She didn't want his restraint, only his passion.

Had she said the words aloud? She was past knowing, beyond caring. There was only the moment, and she cried out, urging him on as he lifted her into his arms, then swept aside the bedcovers and tossed her onto the sheets, shielding her body from his weight as he followed her down.

With one hard, long thrust he entered her, felt the customary tightness as she closed like smooth silk around him, taking him in with a series of tiny gasps at his size.

Never before had he resorted to quite this degree of unbridled savagery. Her gaze clung to his, mesmerised by the primitive hunger that sculpted his features into something wild and untamed. His head was flung back, his neck muscles corded, his jaw clenched.

Then he began to move, slowly at first, almost withdrawing before plunging in, again and again, faster and faster, in a rhythm as old as time.

She became caught up in it, swept along on a roaring tide that crashed, then receded, only to gather force and crash again.

There was only the man, the electrifying primeval emotion, and need.

The control he inevitably maintained was gone, and in its place was something incredibly primitive. A hunger so intense it surpassed passion and became raw desire. Brazen, mesmeric, libidinous.

It was as if she was possessed, held captive by a driven overwhelming need, and she abandoned herself to it, to him, allowing him to take her wherever he chose to lead, exulting in the journey.

She had wondered what it would be like to have him lose all semblance of constraint, to be caught up in his total abandonment. A tiny smile curved the swollen fullness of her mouth. *Wild*, she reflected silently. Incredibly, inexplicably wild.

There was a sense of bewitching satisfaction at having the power to cause a man to lose control so completely in her arms.

Hannah sensed the moment he regained a measure of control, felt the heave of his chest as he dragged in air and steadied his breathing, heard it catch in his throat as his body shuddered in emotive reaction, and she simply held him as he uttered a stream of self-castigating words in whispered Spanish.

She wanted to reassure him, to somehow convey for the first time she truly felt a woman's sensual power, and that she was completely swept away by it.

With a tentative touch, she stroked her fingers lightly over his back, felt the tautened muscles and tense sinew beneath her tactile caress, and attempted to soothe them. Gently she traversed his waist, and traced the rigid outline of his buttocks, squeezing them slightly before trailing slowly up over his ribcage to rest on his shoulders, then capturing his head and bringing his mouth down to hers.

It was she who kissed him, savouring his lips, his mouth, sweeping her tongue in an evocative dance with his, encouraging, beguiling in a brazen invitation.

Afterwards he held her close, his arms a protective cage as he cradled her, and she felt his lips on her hair, at the edge of her cheek, caressing her temple, then nuzzling the soft hollow at the curve of her neck.

'*Madre de Dios,*' Miguel breathed tautly. 'Did I hurt you?'

Hannah pressed her mouth to his throat. 'No.'

It had been passion at its most elemental, for both of them.

His lips found hers, in a kiss that was so incredibly gentle it almost brought her to tears.

'Rest, *amada,*' he bade gently.

She felt the beat of his heart beneath her cheek,

and in the security of his arms she simply closed her eyes and drifted into a dreamless somnolence.

At some stage during the early pre-dawn hours she stirred, felt the lack of human warmth and reached for him, only to find the bed empty. Cautiously she lifted her head and searched the shadowy room. It was then she saw him, silhouetted against the partly drawn curtains, looking out over the shadowed garden.

Slowly she slid from the bed and crossed to stand behind him, aware from his slight movement that he had heard the rustle of the sheets, the almost silent pad of her feet.

Hannah linked her arms around his waist and leaned in against him, holding him close. Long minutes later he gathered her into his arms and carried her into the *en suite*. There, he filled the spa-bath, switched on the jets, then he stepped in and lowered her down in front of him.

She simply closed her eyes and let the pulsing warm water provide a soothing relaxation. It would be so easy just to drift to sleep, and she almost did, only to open her eyes wide when Miguel scooped her out and wrapped her in a huge bath-towel.

Dry, they returned to the bedroom, and she made no protest when he drew her down onto the bed. With exquisite care he began an erotic tasting that took her to the edge of sensual nirvana, then tipped her over.

Would it always be like this? Hannah wondered on the edge of sleep.

Beautiful, glorious, heart-wrenching sex. Affection, fondness, respect. But not love.

She, who had sworn never to become emotionally involved with another man, had no choice.

Her heart belonged to Miguel. It always had, always would, whether he wanted it or not.

CHAPTER SIX

'WONDERFUL,' Elise murmured as she relaxed beneath the canopied section of the comfortable cruiser Miguel had hired for the day.

Hannah adjusted her sunglasses and smiled as Elise pulled the brim of her hat down to shade her face from the sun's strong rays.

Together they'd driven down to Williamstown at ten this morning, where Miguel had organised to hire a luxury cruiser and captain to cruise the sparkling waters, then return mid-afternoon.

'It's nice to get away somewhere quiet,' Elise said appreciatively. 'No phones, no visitors, no one-hundred-and-one things to do.'

And no way a certain very persistent Frenchwoman could intrude, Hannah added silently, unable to prevent herself from wondering what Camille's next move might be.

Miguel and Alejandro were seated at the stern, both casually attired in pale chinos and a polo shirt. Both wore sunglasses and baseball caps, and resembled, Hannah decided, two businessmen relaxing on a rare day off.

All she had to do was *look* at Miguel to feel her insides begin to melt. Traitorous desire flared, and spread stealthily through her body, heating her blood and sensitising every nerve-end into pulsing life.

It was impossible not to relive the cataclysmic passion they'd shared less than twelve hours before, and, as crazy as it seemed, she was willing to swear she could still *feel* him inside her. Sensitive tissues throbbed a little from his possession, and there was a part of her that ached for his touch.

At that moment he turned and cast her a long measured glance, and for an instant she could almost imagine he'd read her mind. Then his mouth curved into a slow, infinitely sensual smile that tore her composure to shreds.

'Lunch,' Elise stated with evident relish, 'might be a good idea.'

'Junior is hungry?' Hannah queried musingly, and found herself laughing at Elise's expression.

'Little missy has very definite ideas on when and what I should eat.' She stood to her feet and smoothed her hands over her barely perceptible bulge. 'Today, I have a craving for ham, mayonnaise, gherkins and pineapple.'

Fortunately Sofia had packed a wide selection into a picnic hamper, together with crunchy bread rolls, salmon, chicken, and a variety of salads.

Hannah went inside the cabin and retrieved the hamper, then with Elise's help she set it out on the table, added bottled water, soft drinks and wine, and called the men to eat.

The fresh air, the faint breeze, made for a very pleasant few hours, and they disembarked and then took the coastal road down to the Port Phillip before returning to Toorak.

A seafood barbecue as the heat of the afternoon sun began to wane completed a relaxing day in good company, and Hannah stacked plates and dishes onto a tray and carried them indoors.

Elise followed her, and together they rinsed and stacked them into the dishwasher in record time.

Hannah wiped down the bench, then paused as Elise touched her arm.

'May I say something?'

'Of course.' Hannah turned and gave Elise her full attention.

'Alejandro had a woman chase him when I was pregnant with our first son. Savannah made a complete nuisance of herself and caused me immeasurable grief at the time.' She smiled a little at the memory. 'Unless I'm reading things wrong, you have a similar nemesis in Camille.' She drew in a deep breath, then released it slowly. 'One thing I learned that might help. The Santanas men are one-woman men.'

'So don't worry about Camille?' Hannah queried wryly.

'Don't worry about Miguel,' Elise corrected gently. Her features momentarily clouded. 'Here we go again,' she groaned, rolling her eyes an instant before she quickly exited the kitchen.

Miguel and Alejandro entered the house as Elise returned from her mercy dash, and Hannah set the coffee filtering as she extracted cups, sugar and milk.

'Tea for me,' Elise requested, and Hannah extracted a tray.

'Why don't you go sit by the pool and I'll bring it out in a few minutes?'

It was pleasant to relax in the quiet evening air and watch the sun go down. The garden lights sprung to life by automatic control, and recessed lighting around the pool area added a luminous glow that was highlighted by underwater pool lighting.

A private fairyland, secluded, peaceful, and a relaxing way to end a lovely day.

Elise voiced the words, and Hannah had to agree.

'Time to go, *querida*,' Alejandro commanded quietly as he stood to his feet. 'You're tired.'

'I am?' Her eyes assumed a musing gleam. 'If you say so.'

How many years had they been married? Hannah posed. Six, seven? Yet the intense passion was there, burning just beneath the surface. Somehow she could imagine it would always be so. Yet it hadn't been in the beginning, she reflected as she stood with Miguel at the front door and watched the tail-lights of their hire car glow in the darkness. An arranged marriage that had gone wrong, with Elise escaping only to find herself involved in a car crash and suffering memory loss.

'More coffee?' Hannah queried as she turned away from the door.

'No,' Miguel refused as he locked up and set the security alarm. 'I need to pack. Alejandro is picking me up at seven-thirty *en route* to the airport.'

Where the Sanmar company Lear jet would fly them across the vast Australian continent to Perth.

Without a word she crossed the foyer with him and ascended the stairs to their room where she watched in silence as Miguel extracted a leather holdall and rapidly tossed in a few shirts, a pair of trousers, together with other essentials.

The thought of him being absent for a few days didn't thrill her at all, and she gathered up a silky nightshirt, then entered the *en suite* to shower.

Miguel joined her there minutes later, and she felt acutely vulnerable as he took the soap from her hand, using it gently over every inch of her body before extending it to her to return the favour.

For a second she hesitated, and the breath caught in her throat as he cupped her face and slanted his mouth down to cover her own in a kiss that was so tender it was all she could do not to cry.

It was a while before they both emerged, and towelled dry, re-entered the bedroom and slipped beneath the covers.

He reached for her, and she went to him willingly, curving her arms round his neck as she pulled his head down to hers.

Miguel indulged her, allowing her to take the initiative, until he stilled her hands and held them.

'*Amante*, no. As much as I want you, last night—'

'Was wonderful,' Hannah assured. 'Earth-shattering.'

'I don't think—'

'Don't,' she pleaded. 'Think, I mean,' she added

quickly. 'Just feel. *Please.*' She extricated her hands and ran light fingers down his chest, traced a pattern over his navel, then moved low. 'I want to make love with you.'

And she did, with exquisite care, rising above him as she took in his length, feeling acute pleasure, enclosing him tightly she began to move.

Yet it was Miguel who took control and measured the pace, making it a slow erotic dance that shattered them both with its intensity. Then he brought her down to him and held her long after her breathing returned to normal and she slept.

Saying goodbye was harder than it had ever been before, and she wanted to say *don't go*. Except the words never found voice, and she managed the semblance of a warm smile as he kissed her briefly before moving quickly out to the car and slipped into the front seat beside Alejandro.

Fortunately there wasn't much time to reflect on Miguel's departure as she returned to the dining room to finish the last of her breakfast and skim the daily newspaper before ascending the stairs to get ready for work.

The replacement salesgirl sent by the agency proved to be a dramatic improvement on Chantal, and Hannah began to relax as the morning progressed.

Renee rang to check how the new girl was shaping up, and Miguel called to say they'd landed in Perth.

When the phone rang again minutes later Hannah

automatically lifted the receiver and intoned her usual greeting.

'*Bonjour*, Hannah.'

The voice on the other end of the phone was familiar. Far too familiar, and not one she wanted to hear.

'How did you get my number?' A silly question, she silently castigated herself the instant the words slipped from her lips.

'Dearest Hannah,' Luc drawled with cynical humour. 'Your boutique has a name, which is listed in the telephone directory.'

The connection to Camille was obvious. 'What do you want?'

'Ah, *chérie*,' he chastised softly. 'Straight to the point.'

'I don't have time to chat.' Her voice was distant, formal.

'Meet me for coffee.'

'I don't think so.'

'You have to break for lunch, surely?'

'Yes, but I don't intend to have it with you.'

'Afraid, *chérie*?'

Had he always been this insufferably arrogant? She almost cringed at the thought she'd once been attracted to him. 'Of you? No.' She replaced the receiver, and turned towards the sheaf of invoices waiting to claim her attention.

A client entered the boutique, and Hannah watched surreptitiously as Elaine moved forward with a practised greeting. In only a matter of hours the girl was showing her worth, and Hannah felt cautiously hopeful she'd work out.

Elaine took a lunch break at midday, and on her return an hour later Hannah crossed the street to the café she usually frequented. The food was good, the coffee superb.

Big mistake, she realised within seconds of entering the busy eatery. Being a creature of habit had its downfall, for anyone familiar with her regular routine would be aware this particular café was her favourite haunt for lunch...whether she chose food to take away, or took the time to eat in.

Seated at a table overlooking the street was Luc Dubois, looking the relaxed urbane sophisticate he aspired to be.

Now why wasn't she surprised to see him there? Luc did nothing without motivation. It made her feel distinctly wary.

'*Bonjour, chérie,*' Luc greeted with deliberate warmth. 'I knew if I sat here long enough it would be only a matter of time before you arrived.'

'I must remember to change my eating venue.' Without a further word she turned on her heel and walked out again.

The entire street held several equally trendy eating places. She'd go somewhere else.

Five minutes later she was seated at a table and had just given her order when someone slid into the seat opposite.

'Whatever the lady ordered,' Luc instructed the waiter, 'make it two.'

Hannah cast him an arctic glare. 'Just what in hell are you trying to pull?'

Luc extended one arm in a sweeping gesture. 'We're in public,' he indicated with an eloquent shrug. 'Why not combine lunch with a little reminiscing?'

Hannah arched one eyebrow. 'To what purpose?'

He tried to look hurt. 'Why, *chérie*. We shared some good times together.'

She spared him a bitter smile. 'It took me three months to discover your charm was only an act.'

'Not all the time.'

'Oh…p-l-e-a-s-e,' she discounted wearily.

'The attraction was Daddy's bank account and my healthy annuity. *I* was irrelevant.' Every instinct told her to get up and walk out *now*.

The waiter delivered two lattes, and against her better judgement she tore open a sugar tube and tipped the contents into the milky froth. Luc did the same.

She cut straight to the chase. 'What has Camille paid you to do?'

He spread both hands in a conciliatory gesture.

'Why should Camille have anything to do with me wanting to share a coffee with you?'

She speared him with a look. 'Don't take me for a fool.'

The waiter arrived with two plates, each containing a salad sandwich. As he turned away a flash bulb exploded nearby, and she caught a brief glimpse of a photographer making a rapid exit.

'Pay dirt,' Luc informed with a cynical smile.

It all clicked into place in an instant, and Hannah rose to her feet in one angry movement, extracted a note from her purse, then flung it down onto the table and walked out into the street.

Dammit, she should have seen it coming! Luc played a tune to the highest bidder. In this instance, Camille. Another step down a diabolical path towards Camille's main goal…Miguel. Now, there was photographic evidence Hannah had shared a meal with Luc. It didn't take a genius to work out how Camille intended to use the photograph.

A car horn blared, and she halted mid-step. Dear God, she whispered shakily as realisation hit that she'd stepped off the footpath onto the road. Get a grip!

Minutes later she entered the boutique, caught Elaine's surprised look, and offered a humourless smile. 'That bad, huh?'

'Are you okay?'

Hannah attempted to downplay the past thirty minutes. 'Something disagreed with me.'

'Or someone?'

'You're good,' Hannah accorded wryly. 'Any problems while I was gone?'

'I sold two shirts, a scarf, and took two orders.'

'Well done.'

'You weren't away long. Did you get to eat?'

'I lost my appetite.' Wasn't that the truth!

It was after six when she arrived home, and she ate the meal Sofia had prepared for her, then she retreated to the study and keyed in the digits to connect with Miguel's mobile, only to get his voice-mail.

Maybe he and Alejandro were out to dinner. She left a message, then took a shower and changed into jeans and a singlet top.

Her mother called, and Hannah accepted an invitation to dinner the following evening. They chatted for a while, catching up on each other's news, and afterwards she watched a television movie before opting to indulge herself by reading in bed.

It was almost eleven when the sudden peal of the telephone startled her into dropping the book, and she caught up the receiver, uttered a brief curse as it slipped from her fingers.

Seconds later she managed an articulate greeting, and heard Miguel's husky voice on the line.

'Did I wake you?'

'No,' Hannah said at once. 'I was reading.'

His soft chuckle set all her fine body hairs standing on end. 'You left a message to call.'

'I—' She hesitated, then opted for the banal. 'How are things going?'

'What is it?' Miguel demanded in a dangerously quiet tone.

'What makes you think something's wrong?'

'Querida,' he drawled with deceptive mildness. 'Don't stall.'

'Luc came into the café opposite the boutique during my lunch break.' She could almost *see* his features harden. 'I refused to join him.'

'There's more to the story?'

'Try having him follow me, sit down at the same

table after I'd ordered, then, just as the waiter delivered the food, a photographer appears from nowhere and captured the two of us apparently sharing a meal.'

'He set you up.'

'I should have seen it coming,' Hannah said wretchedly.

'I'll take care of him.' His voice was tensile steel and just as dangerous.

'What are you going to do?'

Miguel smiled grimly on the other end of the line. 'Ensure he doesn't come near you again.' He waited a beat. 'Or he will answer to me.'

Hannah shivered. 'Miguel—'

'Tomorrow there will be someone to shadow your every move.'

Comprehension dawned. 'I don't need a bodyguard!'

There was a brief silence, then he said hardly, 'My decision, Hannah.'

'Shouldn't it also be mine?'

'Accept it as a protective precaution.'

'And if I choose not to?' she pursued, angered by his high-handedness.

'The bodyguard stays.'

She took a deep breath and released it slowly. 'I don't like tyrannical men.'

'Tough,' Miguel reiterated succinctly. 'Alejandro can wrap up the deal. I'll be on the late afternoon flight Wednesday.'

Now she was getting steamed. 'Don't cut an important business deal short on my account.'

'*You*, *amante*, are more important than any business deal.'

'Me, or my vested interest in the Martinez half of the Sanmar corporation?'

'It's as well the breadth of a continent separates us,' Miguel declared with chilling softness, 'or I would take you to task.'

'For daring to speak the truth?'

She had the distinct impression he was actively controlling his temper. 'It will keep.'

Hannah had had enough. 'Goodnight, Miguel.' She cut the connection, and replaced the receiver.

Overbearing, autocratic man! A *bodyguard*? Was he mad?

She picked up the book and tried to get back into the characters, the story, only to close the cover and toss it down onto the bed.

A protective precaution, indeed! Her teeth worried the soft part of her lower lip. Luc was unlikely to do her physical harm. She doubted he'd risk life or limb or arrest, no matter what price Camille offered him. Or could she be wrong?

It wasn't a comfortable thought, and one that kept her awake long after she'd switched off the bedside lamp.

Dreams invaded her subconscious, a series of scary sequences where she was mysteriously pushed from behind into the path of an oncoming vehicle, and worse, driving a car with brakes that didn't respond when she most needed them.

CHAPTER SEVEN

HANNAH was in the middle of eating breakfast when the 'phone rang, and she answered it on the third ring

'*Buenos días.*' Miguel's faintly accented voice curled round her nerve-ends and tugged at something she was loath to analyse. 'You slept well?'

No, and I missed you like hell. 'Thank you.'

'That's not an answer,' he reproved. Would it help her to know he'd lain awake until almost dawn?

'It's all I'm prepared to give.'

'Be as angry as hell, *querida*,' he warned silkily. 'It won't make any difference.'

'That's an ambiguous statement. I imagine there's a purpose for your call?'

He didn't know whether to laugh or repress the need to wring her neck. 'Remind me to beat you.'

'Lay one hand on me, and I'll...'

'Lost for words?'

'Too many choices,' Hannah reiterated with crushing cynicism.

At the risk of having her hang up on him, he relayed pertinent details of the man he'd hired to take care of her.

'Rodney Spears is thirty-two, ex-police, average height, bulky frame, fair hair, blue eyes. He's driving a late model dark blue Holden sedan.' He gave the registration number. 'He'll be at the house in ten minutes to introduce himself.'

The bodyguard. Hannah clenched the receiver, and threw the cat stretched out on the tiles nearby such a dark look the poor animal leapt to its feet and ran from the room.

'Next you'll tell me he's an expert in unarmed combat and a sharp marksman.'

Miguel didn't answer, which in her mind was an admission by avoidance. 'Apart from the initial introduction this morning, he'll remain unobtrusively in the background. You won't notice him. Nor will anyone else.'

'This is beginning to sound like a scene from a cheap detective movie,' she alluded cynically.

'Indulge me.'

'How long is this subterfuge to continue?'

'For as long as it takes.'

'Do I entertain him for breakfast and dinner?'

Miguel's faint laughter sent goose bumps scudding down her spine. 'He has the days, *querida*. I get to take care of you at night.'

'My guardian angel,' Hannah remarked in droll tones.

'You could thank me.'

'I'm more likely to hit you,' she retaliated fiercely.

'Do you have any plans for tonight?'

'Dinner with my parents.'

'Why don't you stay with them overnight?'

This was too much. *He* was too much! 'I'm way past the age of requiring a babysitter.' She took in a deep breath in an effort to control her anger. 'Aren't you taking this *protection* thing just a bit too far?'

'No,' Miguel declared with hard inflexibility. 'Do as I ask. Please.'

'I'll think about it.'

He wanted to reach down the line and *shake* her. Stubborn independence didn't come close! Yet it was those very qualities he admired in her. But not when he was several thousand miles away.

'I don't want to see you upset or hurt.' His voice deepened slightly. *'Comprende?'*

'Okay, you've made your point,' she conceded, and heard him expel a faint sigh.

'Gracias.'

Sofia escorted a man fitting the bodyguard's description into the breakfast room, and Hannah lowered her voice.

'The cavalry has arrived.'

'I'll call you later.'

He did, and she was able to report Luc hadn't telephoned or shown up at the café.

The day had gone well, with new stock snapped up by various clients. Renee called to say there would be a change of plan and they'd eat at a restaurant.

'I'll go home and change first, then meet you there. Six-thirty?'

Should she alert Rodney Spears? Just as she thought about dialling his mobile, he rang through to confirm her evening plans, and carefully noted the changes.

Hannah checked her rear-vision mirror as she

pulled out from the car park, and glimpsed a dark blue sedan follow at a discreet distance.

Then she lost him in the flow of traffic, and she didn't catch sight of the sedan until an hour later when she left the house *en route* to the restaurant.

It was, she reflected silently, totally unnecessary for him to shadow her every move. When did the man eat, for heaven's sake? Hamburgers and fries at a drive-through? And he had to sleep some time, surely?

Miguel was probably paying him a small fortune, but that didn't stop her from offering Rodney a one-hundred-dollar bill to eat in the restaurant.

'Look on it as a bonus,' she advised when he offered a protest. 'I'll go ahead and ensure you get a table.'

She did, and she'd only been seated a few minutes when Renee and Carlo entered the foyer.

'Darling, have you been waiting long?' Renee greeted anxiously. 'We got held up in traffic.'

It was a pleasant evening. The food was superb, each course presented with flair and artistry. Hannah sipped a half-glass of wine throughout the meal, and together they caught up on each other's news.

'How is Cindy?' Renee broached as she forked a few morsels of salad, then speared a sliver of chicken.

'She was discharged this morning.'

Renee looked at her daughter carefully. 'One imagines Luc's appearance at the Leukaemia Charity Ball was deliberate, rather than a chance circumstance?'

'I have no idea,' Hannah indicated with a slight shrug. 'Nor do I care.'

'It doesn't bother you that he's in town?'

'Why should it? He's a bad memory I'd prefer to forget.'

'He hasn't attempted to contact you?'

'What is this?' she queried lightly. 'The third degree?'

'You would tell us if he proves to be a nuisance?' her father countered insistently.

'He won't get the opportunity.' Her omnipotent husband was taking care of it. She spared a glance towards the bodyguard's table, and saw that he was just finishing up.

She could confide in her parents, but what was the point in worrying them unnecessarily? She opted not to suggest she follow them home and stay overnight. She hadn't done so before on any of the other occasions Miguel had been away. If she suggested it now, their suspicions would be aroused. And what was the point? In her opinion, Miguel's precautions were way over the top. Besides, the house and grounds were secure with a state-of-the-art security system.

When the waiter cleared their plates Hannah declined dessert, the cheeseboard, and settled for coffee. It had been a leisurely meal, and nice to catch up with her parents away from the social scene.

'We should discuss Christmas, darling,' Renee ventured. 'I thought I'd do lunch this year, and invite Esteban.'

Christmas? Why, that was—

'Nine weeks away, darling,' her mother reminded. 'The first of the pre-Christmas social festivities begins next week.'

Heavens, it was that close? 'I'll check with Miguel, but I'm sure lunch will be fine.'

'Well, this is a nice surprise.'

Hannah heard her father's words an instant before she felt a hand touch her shoulder.

'What will you check with me, *querida*?'

She turned her head at the sound of that deep, faintly accented drawl, and felt the floor drop away.

Miguel?

'I didn't expect you back until tomorrow night,' she managed an instant before his mouth closed over hers in a brief, tantalising kiss. The quick sweep of his tongue wreaked havoc with her senses, and it took a few seconds to regain her scattered thoughts.

Why was he *here* at this restaurant?

'I caught a taxi from the airport.'

'Have you eaten?' Renee queried warmly as he took the chair next to Hannah.

'On the plane,' Miguel confirmed. 'However, I'll join you for coffee.' He caught hold of her hand and lifted it to his lips, then he linked his fingers through her own and rested them on his thigh.

His smile left her breathless, the faint teasing quality stirring her emotions to fever pitch within seconds.

'What will you check with me?' he repeated, giving Hannah his total attention.

It wasn't fair that one man should possess such

devastating sensuality, or that she could be rendered so intensely vulnerable by his look, his touch.

From somewhere she restored order to her scattered thoughts. 'Christmas. Renee mentioned lunch, if it suits your father to join us for dinner.'

How did Miguel know she'd be dining at this restaurant?

Rodney Spears, Hannah concluded. The bodyguard had obviously reported the change in venue to Miguel. But what had occurred to influence Miguel to drop everything and fly home at a moment's notice?

Whatever it was, it had to wait until they were alone, and she toyed with her coffee, stirring it unnecessarily, then she sipped the contents without registering the excellent espresso blend.

The next hour seemed to be one of the longest in her life, and she breathed an inward sigh of relief when Miguel indicated they would leave.

Hannah burst into speech the instant they were inside the car, and Miguel effectively silenced her by placing a hand over her mouth.

'It'll keep until we get home.' He put the car in gear and reversed out before heading towards the exit.

'The hell it will,' she said fiercely as he joined the flow of traffic and headed towards Toorak.

Miguel slanted her a long glance as he drew to a temporary halt at a set of lights. 'The thought that I might have cut my trip short just to be here with you does not please you?'

'I'm still mad at you over the bodyguard bit.' She

met his gaze and held it, then the lights changed and he gave the road his attention. 'I take it I have Rodney to thank for reporting to you my every move?'

'That's what I pay him to do.'

'A case of total overkill.'

'You may change your mind when you see what I have to show you.'

Something in his tone stilled the retort she was about to utter. A cold hand closed round her heart, and she searched his features, noting the hard set of his jaw, the serious expression which didn't bode well.

'It's Camille, isn't it?' Hannah queried quietly. 'What has she done?'

Miguel turned the car into their driveway, paused while the electronically controlled gates swung open, then he headed towards the house. Within minutes he entered the garage and cut the engine.

He popped the boot and removed a bag and his briefcase. 'Let's go indoors, shall we?'

He led her into the study, dropped his bag to the floor, then he placed the briefcase on the desk, unlocked it, and extracted a large manila envelope.

'A scanned copy of these was sent to me by e-mail today.' He withdrew six colour prints and spread them out on the desk. 'Look at them carefully.'

There was no mistaking the first three prints. They featured herself and Luc sharing lunch. The second three prints were something else entirely.

Miguel and Camille seated at a table together.

Worse, they were looking into each other's eyes with an expression only lovers shared.

Hannah felt sick, and it was all she could do to regulate her breathing. Dear heaven. Miguel and *Camille*?

'Look at them very carefully, *querida*,' Miguel prompted gently. He was almost afraid to touch her for fear she might shatter. A silent rage reasserted itself, and he consciously held it in check. 'They are not quite what they seem.'

'They look real enough to me.'

'As they are meant to.' He picked up one print and pointed to Camille. 'If you look very carefully, you will see there is a slight difference in the reflection of light.' He picked up a pen and pointed its tip to the print. 'Here. Do you see?'

The texture wasn't quite the same, the shade of light reflecting from one set of features compared to the other was fractionally different.

'The original photograph has been digitally enhanced on a computer. In this particular print your image has been removed, and Camille's image superimposed. I had it checked out.' He picked up a sheet of paper and handed it to her. 'This report confirms it.'

Hannah was silent as she examined the prints again, then she read the in-depth report noting the technical irregularities.

'What do you think Camille's next step will be?' she queried slowly, trying to dispel the ache that had settled round her heart.

'At a guess, Camille will ensure you receive the second set of prints some time tomorrow.'

'Delivered personally, with verbal embellishment.' Hannah predicted. 'Will she take it further, do you think?'

Miguel arched one eyebrow. 'The media? She may try. However, these prints will never be used.' He had influence, and a copy of the technician's report had already been faxed to various sources.

'I owe you an apology.'

He took the prints and the report from her hand and locked them in his briefcase.

'For what, precisely?'

'Accusing you of overreacting,' Hannah said simply. 'And I want to thank you for ensuring I saw those—' she indicated his briefcase '—before Camille dredged every ounce of shock value from them tomorrow.'

She died a thousand deaths just thinking about it.

Miguel lifted a hand and trailed his fingers down her cheek. 'Camille is about to learn I will not tolerate any form of invasion.'

She looked at him, taking in his strength, the power he exuded, and felt infinitely relieved she wasn't his enemy. 'I see.'

His mouth curved slightly. 'Do you?'

'Yes.' It was all about preserving the image, professionally and personally. She told herself she understood. Hadn't she been reared to be aware of *image*? The private-school education, extra-curricular activities, the social niceties? Luc had been her only transgression...if believing the false words of a cad could be termed a transgression.

'I doubt that you do,' Miguel denied silkily. 'Verbal abuse is difficult to prove without an independent witness. So is slander.' His expression hardened. 'However, these prints and the report prove Camille's intent to defame.'

'You intend to confront her?'

'Not personally.' His voice was clipped, he was watching her expressive features. 'In the only way she will understand.'

'Legal action?'

'Yes.'

There was a ruthlessness apparent that boded ill for anyone daring to cross him, and Hannah shivered, caught up in a mix of complex emotions.

He wanted it done. Camille and her obsessive behaviour out of their lives. As to Luc... It would be as well if he never caught sight of him again. To do so would incite the possibility of physical assault, he decided grimly.

Hannah took in a deep breath, then released it. 'What do you want me to do?'

'Nothing. Absolutely nothing, do you understand? We must wait for her next move.' His gaze speared hers, dark and incredibly formidable. 'No heroics, Hannah. Rodney Spears will be close at all times.'

Miguel reached forward and caught hold of her shoulders, sliding his hands down her back as he pressed her body close in against his own. He angled his head and nuzzled her earlobe, then feathered a trail of kisses down the edge of her neck. 'Miss me?'

Dear heaven, *yes*. She didn't like sleeping alone in their bed. She'd turn over in her sleep, subconsciously searching for the warmth of his body, seeking the touch of his hands, the reassuring brush of his lips...only to discover a cool empty space.

'Uh-huh.' His mouth was playing havoc with her senses. The blood sang in her veins, heating all the pleasure pulses and creating a fast-pacing tempo that demanded more, much more than the touch of his lips.

Hannah gave a faint gasp as an arm skimmed beneath her knees and Miguel lifted her against his chest. Her eyes were almost on a level with his own as he carried her into the foyer and began ascending the stairs.

She saw the passion smouldering in those dark depths and felt the thrill of anticipated pleasure as he gained the gallery and strode towards their bedroom.

When he lowered her down to her feet she simply wound her arms round his neck and brought his mouth down to her own.

She was hardly aware of him divesting her of her clothes, or that her fingers dispensed with shirt buttons, took care of his belt and the zip on his trousers.

There was only the need to feel skin on skin, the ecstasy of their joined bodies moving in perfect harmony as they created the ultimate pleasure.

Something they sought and achieved again in the

early dawn hours before sleep claimed them for a brief hour.

The need to rise and face the new day saw them shower, dress, share breakfast and depart the house in separate cars *en route* to their respective places of business.

CHAPTER EIGHT

How long would it take Camille to stage her confrontation?

It had to be today, Hannah estimated, for if the Frenchwoman had gone to such pains to discover Miguel's plans, she'd be aware he was due to return home tonight.

Anticipating the time and place made her edgy, and by midday she was fast becoming a nervous wreck. It made sense that Camille would choose a time when Hannah was alone, which meant the hour Elaine went on lunch break, or immediately afterwards when Hannah visited the café.

Knowing Rodney Spears remained unobtrusively on duty provided reassurance.

Hannah checked her watch, and indicated Elaine should go to lunch, during which the phone rang three times, three clients called in to collect orders, two people opted to browse, and Camille was a no-show.

The nervous tension mounted with every passing minute as she ordered a Caesar salad and carrot juice at the café counter, paid, then selected one of three empty tables and took a seat.

The salad was delectable, she knew, because she frequently ordered the dish. However, today she could have been eating chalk, and her appetite was non-existent.

Hannah sat there for more than half an hour, then she ordered bottled water and slowly sipped it over the next fifteen minutes. Camille was nowhere to be seen.

At ten to two, Hannah walked out onto the street, visited a nearby newsagent and selected a card to send to Cindy, then she retraced her steps to the boutique.

Elaine left at four, and an hour later Hannah checked the locks, set the alarm, closed up and walked to the car park.

She slid into the Porsche and closed the door, inserted the key into the ignition, then gasped in shocked surprise as the door opened from the outside.

Camille leant forward and dropped a large envelope onto her lap. 'I thought you should have these.' She stood back and prepared to close the door. 'By the way, Perth was fun, darling.'

Where had she come from? Hannah questioned silently. Then she heard the sound of an engine, and she turned to see Camille behind the wheel of a car as it moved quickly towards the exit.

Seconds later Rodney Spears appeared out of nowhere. 'Are you okay?'

'I'm fine.'

He didn't appear convinced. 'I'll report in to Mr Santanas.'

Hannah tried for a smile, and almost made it.

Rodney Spears had already hit the rapid dial key and was talking into the phone. 'The perpetrator dropped off a package. One minute contact. Yes, your wife is fine. I'll follow her home.' He cut the connection. 'Are you okay to go now, ma'am?'

She was about as okay as she would ever be. 'Sure.' Seconds later she cleared the exit and joined the line of cars crawling along Toorak Road.

Perth? Why had Camille mentioned Perth?

It took several minutes to reach the turn-off, and she moved freely through various residential streets before entering her own.

Miguel's Jaguar was parked outside the front door, and she drew the Porsche to a halt behind it.

No sooner had she entered the foyer than he was there, tall and brooding, his eyes compellingly dark as he raked her petite frame.

His gaze shifted to the large envelope in her hand, and he took it from her, then he cupped her chin and kissed her, hard.

'Let's take this into the study.' Miguel caught hold of her hand and led the way. 'I think we could both do with a drink.'

And then some, Hannah echoed silently as she entered the large book-lined room, watching as he opened a bottle of chilled white wine and filled two goblets with the golden liquid.

She accepted one and took a long sip of the contents as he leaned one hip against the desk.

Hannah indicated the envelope. 'Aren't you going to open that?'

'In a minute. First, there's something you need to know.'

She held his gaze, then said slowly, 'I don't think I want to hear this.'

'Camille apparently discovered I would be in Perth, and she not only caught an earlier flight, she also booked into the same hotel.'

He caught the fleeting stricken look before she successfully controlled it, and he felt moved to violence at the lengths Camille was prepared to go to wreak destruction.

'Don't tell me,' Hannah said bitterly. 'Not only does that envelope contain doctored photographs we've already seen, but shots taken of the hotel with the date function exposed.' Her gaze lanced his. 'What else? You leaving your hotel room? Camille posing in the hallway with the room number showing, should I want to check it out?'

'Worse. Camille lying almost naked in an unmade bed. The fact it isn't *my* bed is immaterial, as most of the rooms are identical.'

She stood up and carefully placed the goblet down onto the desk. *Calm*, a tiny voice soothed. Stay calm. Just go look at the prints. Examine them carefully. And don't say a word until you're done.

With slow deliberation she slit the edge of the envelope and extracted the prints. One by one she discarded them onto the desk until she came to the final six.

As she anticipated, there was a photo taken of the hotel exterior, another of the reception area with a clear view of Camille checking in. The hallway, displaying a room number on the door. Miguel emerging from the same room. And the final two showing Camille sprawled in differing poses among rumpled sheets looking dreamily sated and incredibly seductive.

Hannah's first inclination was to rip them in half and throw them in the waste bin. It sickened her to look at them, and she felt positively ill at the mental image of Miguel pleasuring another woman. Even if it hadn't happened, just the thought was enough to kill her.

'Look at the date.'

Miguel's voice penetrated the dark void into which she'd mentally retreated, and she shook her head.

'*Por Dios.*' The husky imprecation sounded like silk being razed by razor-sharp steel. '*Look.*'

It was today's date. *Today?* But—

'I was here last night,' Miguel relayed inexorably. 'With you.'

Irrefutable proof. 'Just as well,' Hannah ventured with a shaky smile. 'Otherwise I'd have killed you, or worse.'

He appeared vaguely amused. 'Then it's fortunate I have an alibi for Monday evening.'

'I hope it's watertight.'

'It is. Alejandro will confirm.' His voice became hard, his expression inflexible. 'Camille will be served with an interim injunction. If she chooses to disregard it, she'll be charged, independently of existing harassment charges.' He paused fractionally. 'Then there's scientific proof regarding tampering of photographic prints.' His gaze speared hers. 'If she's wise, she'll take the first flight out of here.'

And their lives would revert to normal. Until the next time, Hannah added cynically. Although many women coveted Miguel, none had gone to such extraordinary lengths as Camille. Because the woman was obsessive? A practised man-stealer who derived her satisfaction from setting the scene and playing a devious game?

It made Hannah feel fiercely territorial. And possessive. About Miguel, her marriage, her home... *everything* she held sacred.

There were a few what if's tumbling around in her mind, and she felt sickened at the thought that Camille's plan had almost worked.

Don't go there, she silently cautioned. A partnership, a marriage, had to be built on trust. If there wasn't trust, there was nothing.

She reached for her goblet and took a generous sip of wine. It curled round her stomach and seeped into her veins, gradually lessening the tension.

A few weeks ago she hadn't known of Camille Dalfour's existence. Yet in the past week the Frenchwoman had managed to create chaos.

Miguel could take whatever action he chose. But *she* intended to instigate a strategy of her own.

In an impulsive move she drained the remaining wine in a long swallow, then replaced the empty goblet down onto the desk.

'I feel like a swim before dinner.'

Miguel let her go, and when the door closed behind

her he slid the prints back into the envelope and locked them in the wall safe. Then he picked up the phone and dialled his lawyer's number.

Hannah slipped out of her clothes and stepped into a stunning deep aqua one-piece, then she pinned up her hair, snagged a towel and ran lightly down the stairs.

The pool looked inviting, the water clear and sparkling in the early evening sunlight. The heat of the day had diminished slightly, but it was still hot, and she dived cleanly in at the deep end and when she surfaced she struck out with leisurely strokes, one lap after another, until she'd counted to fifty, then she turned onto her back and lay there, held buoyant by the crystal water.

She could feel the sun on her face, her limbs, and she closed her eyes, becoming lost in reflective thought.

Soon she would need to emerge, go upstairs, shower and change ready for dinner. But, for now, she was bent on enjoying the quietness and the solitude.

Five minutes later she rolled onto her stomach in one fluid movement and made her way to the tiled ledge.

The strategy took shape as she showered, then she dried her hair and slipped into a casual pencil-slim skirt and top. Minimum make-up, a touch of lipstick and she was ready.

Dinner was timed for six-thirty, and a quick glance

at her watch revealed she had just five minutes to set the plan in motion.

Rather than use the house line, she extracted her cell-phone and punched in a series of numbers.

'Graziella?' She exchanged pleasantries, then voiced her request. 'Could I speak to Camille, if she's there?'

If Camille was surprised at the identity of her caller, she didn't show it.

'Hannah, how charming, *chérie*.' Her tone was pure feline.

'Let's do lunch tomorrow.' Hannah named an up-market restaurant a block from the boutique. 'One o'clock. Be there.' She cut the connection before Camille had a chance to utter a further word.

Dinner was a simple meal of chicken served with piquant rice and a delectable salad with fresh fruit to follow. Hannah declined wine in favour of a lemon spritzer, and admired Miguel's appetite while she merely picked at the food on her plate.

'Not hungry?'

She met Miguel's steady gaze and effected a light shrug. 'A client brought in a platter of fresh grapes, crackers and cheese. Elaine and I nibbled all after-noon.'

'You haven't forgotten we have tickets for the opening of David Williamson's new play tomorrow night?'

She'd been so preoccupied with Camille, she hadn't checked her social diary for days. 'No, of course not.'

'I have some work to do on the laptop for an hour or so,' Miguel declared as Hannah pushed her plate to one side.

'Likewise.' End-of-month invoices, stock receipts, and she also needed to check catalogues from several different fashion houses. 'I should make a start on it.'

'You load the dishwasher,' he instructed, rising to his feet. 'I'll make coffee.'

There was a part of her that wanted the comfort of his touch, the warmth of his arms and the feel of his mouth on hers. In reassurance? It didn't help to feel this needy. Yet they shared a marriage, had created a bond, and what more natural than to go to him, wind her arms round his neck and pull his head down to hers?

She couldn't do it. Not here, not now. Camille stood like a spectre between them, a living, breathing entity that seemed to sap her natural warmth and spontaneity.

When the coffee was made, she poured it into two cups and carried hers through to the comfortable room next to Miguel's study. It wasn't as large as his, but it held an antique desk, bookshelves, filing cabinet, and a laptop.

For the next two hours she worked diligently, and when the paperwork was up to date she fired off a few e-mails to friends, which mostly took care of personal correspondence.

'Not finished yet?'

Hannah looked up and saw Miguel's tall frame leaning against the door-jamb. He'd removed cuff-links and rolled back his shirt-sleeves. The top few buttons on his shirt were loosened, and he looked as if he'd raked fingers through his hair more than once.

'Five minutes.'

'Want to watch a video?'

Why not? 'Okay.'

'Comedy? Action? Drama?'

She wrinkled her nose and gave him an impish grin. 'Surprise me.'

When she entered the entertainment room he sat sprawled on the leather couch, a half-magnum of chilled champagne rested in an ice-bucket, there was a packet of crisps waiting to be opened, the lights were dimmed, and the television screen was running previews prior to the main movie.

Miguel patted the space beside him and extended a hand. His eyes were dark and his mouth curved into a sensual smile. 'Come here.'

'That sounds like an invitation,' she murmured as she crossed the room, and his smile broadened.

'Do you need one?'

Hannah indicated the ice-bucket. 'Are we celebrating?'

He caught hold of her hand and pulled her down to him. He leaned forward, eased the cork from the bottle, then poured the contents into two flutes and handed her one. *'Salut.'*

Miguel took a sip of excellent vintage champagne and watched as she mirrored his action, then he took the flute from her hand and gave her his.

It was a deliberately sensual gesture, and she held

his gaze for a few seconds, all too aware of the exigent sexual chemistry between them.

Liquid fire coursed through her veins, awakening each separate sensory nerve-end until her body became one pulsing ache in anticipation of his touch.

With considerable effort she dragged her gaze away and looked blindly at the television screen, focusing on the Technicolor images as the movie began to unfold.

The champagne was superb and she sipped the contents slowly, aware of the shift in Miguel's frame as he draped an arm along the back of the couch bare inches above her shoulders.

It was a relationship film, the acting excellent, and if she remembered correctly both male and female leads had earned Oscar nominations for the parts they played.

Hannah gradually became absorbed in the plot, and relaxed a little. She finished her champagne and Miguel took the empty flute from her fingers, placed it on a nearby low table, then settled back.

Minutes later she was aware of his fingers playing idly with her hair, gradually loosening the pins that held the smooth twist neatly together.

Her concentration was shot to hell as he leaned close and nuzzled her earlobe, then began pressing light kisses along the edge of her neck. When he savoured the sensitive hollow at its base, it was all she could do not to groan out loud.

'You want to see this movie?' she questioned huskily, and heard his soft chuckle.

'You watch it, *querida*.' His fingers slipped open one shirt button and slid beneath her lacy bra to tease one burgeoning peak. 'I have something else in mind.'

'Here?'

A hand covered her thigh and began a slow upward slide. 'We'll eventually make the bedroom.' He released another shirt button. 'But for now, enjoy.'

Five minutes was all it took for her to twist her fingers into the folds of his shirt and pull him hard against her. It was her mouth that sought his with hungry passion, eliciting a husky chuckle as his arms bound her close.

With urgent hands she sought his waist, wrenching the buckle open in her quest to touch him as he had caressed her.

She felt shameless, utterly wanton, in the need for his possession, and she gasped as he reared to his feet in one easy movement and strode towards the stairs.

On reaching the bedroom they helped remove each other's clothes, then Miguel took her down onto the bed with him and subjected her to such exquisite lovemaking she wept from the joy of it.

Later, much later, it was she who initiated a slow, sensual journey that had him breathing deeply as he fought for control, only to lose it as she rode him to a tumultuous climax that left their bodies slick with sensual sweat and sated emotions.

CHAPTER NINE

THE day began with rain, which diminished to light showers and by midday the city was bathed in steamy heat and high humidity.

Hannah had dressed to kill in a tailored lightweight black suit that shrieked *class*. The deep V of the buttoned jacket showed a tantalising glimpse of cleavage. Black stiletto-heeled shoes added extra height to her petite frame and sheer black stockings showcased slender calves. Her hair was smoothed into a sleek chignon, and she wore minimum jewellery.

The overall look was one of a woman who was self-confident with high self-esteem. It hardly mattered that inside she felt like jelly as she entered the chosen restaurant a deliberate few minutes late.

It appeared Camille intended to play the same game, for she was nowhere in sight, and Hannah allowed the *maître d'* to escort her to a reserved table where she ordered a light spritzer and sipped it slowly as the minutes ticked on.

The waiting increased her nervous tension, and after ten minutes she summoned the waiter and placed her order. If Camille intended to be a no-show—

'Hannah. My apologies.' The voice was as fake as the smile Camille offered as she slid into the seat opposite. 'I was held up on the phone.' She lifted a

hand in an expressive Gallic gesture. 'Parking, you
know how it is.'

Begin as you mean to go on, a tiny voice prompted.
'I've already ordered. I can only spare an hour.'

The wine steward appeared and Camille ordered
Dom Perignon. 'I thought we'd celebrate, darling.'

'And the occasion is?' Hannah queried with a lift
of one eyebrow.

'Why—*life.*' Camille's smile didn't reach her eyes.
'Isn't that enough reason?'

'Not,' she countered firmly, 'when you're determined to interfere in mine.'

The waiter presented the menu and Camille spared
it the briefest of glances, ordered a salad, then flipped
Hannah a hard, calculated look. 'Haven't you learnt
I am a formidable adversary?'

'A very foolish one.'

Camille's gaze narrowed. 'What did you think of
the prints, darling?'

'The digitally altered ones?' Hannah posed silkily.
'Or the few of you sprawled among the sheets in a
state of *déshabillé*?'

The calculation evident intensified into something
that was almost dangerous. 'How else would I be,
when Miguel had just left my bed?'

'Wrong, Camille,' she corrected with deceptive
quietness. 'Miguel was never in your bed.'

Camille's expression didn't change. 'Failing to face
up to reality, darling?'

Hannah speared a succulent asparagus, dipped the
tip in the river of hollandaise sauce on her plate, and

took time to savour it. 'It is *you* who needs a reality check,' she offered seconds later.

'The prints were explicit.'

She looked at the Frenchwoman, and almost felt sorry for her. 'A fantasy, Camille.'

Camille's lips tightened. 'Irrefutable proof. The date function does not lie.'

'No,' Hannah agreed. 'You made just one small mistake.'

'And what was that?'

She took her time in answering. 'Miguel flew home Tuesday evening.'

'Impossible. The suite was still occupied.'

'By Alejandro,' she confirmed. 'You were just too clever in activating the camera date function. It made a mockery of Miguel being in your bed, when he was already in mine.'

'What of Monday night, Hannah?' Camille queried hatefully, and Hannah fought back the desire to slap the Frenchwoman's cheek.

'Camille, give it up. You played what you thought was your trump card, and it proved to be the joker.'

Red lacquered nails on one hand curled round the table napkin. 'You invited me to lunch to tell me this?'

'No,' she denied. 'I wanted the opportunity to warn you in person that I won't tolerate your attempts to interfere in my life, or my marriage.'

Camille pressed a hand against the region of her heart. 'I am so afraid.'

The degree of dramatic mockery was almost laughable, if Hannah was inclined to see humour in the situation. 'Be afraid,' she warned inflexibly. 'I can have you charged with harassment and stalking.' Her gaze was direct, her tone icy with intent. She waited a beat, then added, 'I doubt your aunt will be impressed. Nor, I imagine, will Graziella and Enrico del Santo.'

Camille's eyes glittered with dark malevolence.

'I am not finished with you yet. Miguel—'

'Finds you as much of a nuisance as I do,' Hannah intercepted smoothly. 'Go get a life, Camille. And get out of mine.'

A venomous stream of French issued from Camille's perfectly outlined mouth in a pithy, street-gutter diatribe that left those who comprehended the language in little doubt of an attack on Hannah's parentage, status and character.

Two things happened simultaneously, and Hannah had the briefest warning of both.

Camille's hand snaked out and caught her cheek a stinging slap. Champagne spilled across the damask tablecloth. Then Rodney Spears appeared from nowhere and held the Frenchwoman's flailing arms in a restraining grip.

What happened next was almost comedic, as the waiter almost flew to the table, followed close on his heels by the *maître d'*. Fellow patrons looked alarmed, others merely curious, and throughout it all Camille continued to demean every one of Hannah's relatives, both living and those who had passed on.

It almost contained a surreal quality, like something out of a movie.

'You wish me to call the police, *madame*?' the *maître d'* queried with concern. He was all too aware of Hannah's identity and her connection to two of the city's wealthiest families.

Hannah ignored Rodney Spears' nod of assent. 'No.'

'You are sure, *madame*?' he repeated anxiously. 'You are not hurt?'

The left side of her face stung, emotionally she was a little shaken up, but that was all. 'I'm fine.'

'There will, of course, be no charge for the meal. Can I get you something to drink?'

'I will take care of Mrs Santanas,' Rodney asserted in a tone that brooked no argument. 'Just as soon as I have escorted this woman from the premises.'

He shot Hannah a direct look. 'You are quite sure you don't want her detained?'

She turned towards Camille, who resembled a spitting cat waiting for another opportunity to lash out. 'Come within ten metres of me again, and I'll slap you with every charge in the book,' she warned with quiet dignity. Difficult, when inside she felt like a nervous wreck.

Rodney strong-armed the Frenchwoman from the restaurant, and Hannah viewed the table, the spilled champagne, the scattered food.

'I apologise,' she offered simply, and had her words immediately waved aside. She gathered up her purse and withdrew her credit card.

'No, no, *madame*.' He waved aside the card. 'There is no need to leave. Let me arrange another meal.'

'Thank you, but I must get back to work.' She had to get out of here and breathe in some fresh air.

'You should wait for the detective to return.'

The bodyguard. Oh, hell, that meant Rodney would report to Miguel, and then, she grimaced, there would be hell to pay.

It didn't take long. Ten minutes, Hannah counted, checking her watch as her cell-phone rang.

'What in *hell* are you playing at?' Miguel demanded the instant she acknowledged the call.

'Protecting my own turf,' she relayed imperturbably, and heard his soft curse.

'Don't be facetious.'

'The cavalry arrived just in time.'

'Hannah,' he growled. 'I am far from being amused.'

'I wasn't exactly laughing, myself.'

'Close the boutique and go home.'

'Why? I'm fine.'

'Hannah—'

'If you must conduct a post-mortem, it can wait until tonight.'

The answering silence was palpable, and she could almost *hear* him summoning control. 'Tonight,' he conceded hardly. 'Meantime, Rodney stays close. *Comprende?*'

Rodney's instructions were explicit, for he took *close* to mean his presence inside the boutique in full view of any clientele who happened to wander in and peruse the stock.

Elaine was fascinated by the drama, concerned at the reddened patch on Hannah's cheek, applied an ice-pack, and insisted on staying until closing time.

Of Camille there was neither sign nor word, and Hannah suffered Rodney escorting her to the car park, then following so close behind his bumper was almost touching her car.

Miguel greeted her at the door, and she cast him an exasperated look as he took her face between both hands and conducted a tactile examination of the affected cheek.

There was a slight bruise just beginning to appear over the cheekbone, and his gentle probing made it difficult not to wince.

'Talk to me,' Miguel commanded. 'Does it hurt when you move your jaw?'

She effected a light shrug, and saw his gaze narrow. 'Not too much.'

He took hold of her arm and led her into the study, closed the door, then he turned to face her.

'Now, suppose you tell me how you happened to lunch with Camille?'

Oh, my, the third degree. The simple truth was the only way to go. 'I rang and invited her.'

His features assumed a brooding study. Without a word he crossed to the desk and leaned a hip against its edge.

'What in heaven's name possessed you to do that?'

The query was silk-smooth and dangerous, and she viewed him with open defiance.

'I tired of being a victim. Camille was running all the action. I figured it was about time she was told enough was enough.'

'Even knowing I had already instigated legal action and the matter was in hand?' His gaze was direct and analytical. 'Aware,' he continued with an infinite degree of cynicism, 'that the woman was unpredictable, and therefore dangerous?'

'I wasn't alone with her,' Hannah defended. 'And, thanks to you, the inestimable Rodney was on hand.'

His gaze speared hers. 'Did it occur to you what might have happened if he hadn't been there?'

She drew herself up to her full height and glared at him. 'If you're done with the inquisition, I'm going to have a shower and change.'

Miguel uncoiled his length and reached her before she had taken more than a step. His hands closed over her shoulders, then he cupped her chin and tilted her head. 'Give me your word there'll be no more attempts at independent heroics.'

He was close, much too close. A pulse thudded at the base of her throat, and she just stood still, looking at him as he examined her features with daunting scrutiny.

The breath seemed to catch in her throat, and her eyes clung to his, bright, angry, yet intensely vulnerable. 'I'll give it some thought.'

His husky imprecation acted like a catalyst.

'Are you done?' She tried to wrench away from him and failed. 'Let me go, damn you!'

His eyes assumed an inexorable bleakness. 'Dinner will be ready in half an hour.' He brushed the pad of his thumb along her lower lip, felt it quiver, and wanted to *shake* her. 'We're due at the theatre at seven-thirty.'

Oh, Lord. She almost groaned out loud. The play. The producer was a personal friend. Not to appear would be the height of impoliteness.

'I'm not hungry.'

Emotional upheaval and nerves were hell and damnation. Heaven knew she'd experienced enough of both in the past week to last her for ages.

'If you're not in the dining room in half an hour, I'll come get you.'

Her eyes widened, deepening to a brilliant sapphire. 'Don't play the heavy husband,' she warned, and saw his eyes harden.

'Hannah.' His voice held a silky warning she chose not to heed.

'Don't,' she retaliated angrily. 'Just—*don't*.'

Miguel released her without a further word, and she walked from the room.

A leisurely shower did much to restore her equilibrium, and, donning fresh underwear, she pulled on smart jeans and a top, blow-dried her hair, then she went downstairs.

Sofia had prepared a succulent beef stew with crunchy bread rolls and a salad. The pervasive aroma tempted Hannah's appetite, and she ate with enjoyment.

She thought of a few topics of conversation, then abandoned each of them.

'Nothing to say?'

She glanced at him, met his gaze and held it, then she forked some rice and speared a plump prawn. 'What would you suggest? My contretemps with Camille has been done to death.'

'Renee rang. She assured me it was of no importance, and indicated she'll have the opportunity to speak with you tonight.'

Hannah looked at him sharply. 'You didn't tell her about today?'

'No. Why would I worry her unnecessarily?'

Her mother would freak if she discovered the extent of Camille's campaign and the repercussions it had caused.

Opening night at the theatre meant dressing up, and Hannah chose an ensemble that comprised a high-waisted skirt with alternating bands of cyclamen-pink and burnt orange and a strapless fitted top in burnt orange. A long wrap in cyclamen-pink completed the outfit, and she selected minimum jewellery, choosing to twist her hair into a fashionable knot atop her head.

Members of the city's social élite were in attendance, and it came as no surprise to discover Graziella and Enrico del Santo mingling among the guests in the auditorium. Also present were their friends, Aimee Dalfour, *and*, Hannah noted, Camille and Luc.

Somehow, the 'cat among the pigeons' allegory

didn't even begin to cover it. Admittedly, the harassment injunction Miguel had applied for wouldn't be served until the following day, but, given Camille was no fool, her appearance here tonight was nothing short of blatant arrogance.

Dressed to kill, the Frenchwoman looked positively sinful in a designer gown that was strapless, backless, and moulded her curves like a second skin.

A last-ditch attempt to show Miguel what he was missing?

Impossible, of course, that they could slip through the foyer unnoticed. Nor could they ignore the del Santos' presence.

Act, Hannah prompted silently as Miguel enfolded her hand within his own.

'Hannah, Miguel. How nice to see you,' Graziella greeted with enthusiasm. 'You remember Aimee, of course. Camille, Luc.'

How could they forget? They exchanged polite meaningless pleasantries and Hannah endeavoured to ignore Camille's sultry appraisal of Miguel. It was a wonder he didn't *burn* at the sensual pouting of her lips and the wicked promise portrayed in the provocative depths of her gaze.

If they were seated close together, she'd *scream,* Hannah decided, and was immeasurably relieved to see her parents moving towards them.

'Oh, my,' Renee murmured minutes later as the del Santo party moved away. 'Is there an apt word for such exhibitionism?'

'Not one utterable in polite company,' Hannah acknowledged with a touch of cynical amusement.

Within minutes the auditorium doors were opened, and the guests began making their way forward to take up reserved seating. Hannah attempted to extricate her hand from Miguel's firm clasp, and failed. Was he making a statement, or seeking to provide her with reassurance? Maybe both?

Hell, now she was being paranoid!

As they took their seats she was thankful there was no sign of the del Santo party within the immediate vicinity, and she began to relax.

The play was superbly acted, the sets, the characters magnificent, and Hannah took pleasure in losing herself in the excellence of the script, the cast, the production.

The interval provided the opportunity for patrons to mix and mingle in the foyer, have a drink or coffee at the bar, or choose to remain in their seats.

'Let's go out for coffee, shall we?' Renee suggested. 'Miguel and Carlo can opt for something stronger—' she flashed Hannah a conspiratorial smile '—while we check out the fashions other women are wearing.'

Why not? Hannah rose to her feet and felt the light touch of Miguel's hand at the back of her waist as they moved into the aisle.

His close proximity stirred her senses, and she felt the return of nervous tension as they entered the foyer.

There were people she knew, a few clients and their

partners, friends, and she paused briefly to exchange a greeting as they crossed to the bar.

'Renee, Carlo. Please join us.'

Hannah momentarily closed her eyes, then opened them again. Enrico del Santo indicated four chairs empty at their table. This was not her evening! How long did the interval last? Ten to fifteen minutes? She could survive that long in Camille and Luc's company, surely?

Miguel deliberately placed Hannah next to Renee and took the adjoining seat. He was charming to Graziella, conversed with Carlo and Enrico, and chose a polite façade whenever Camille commanded his attention.

A frequent occurrence, Hannah noticed, as she was meant to. It all became a bit much, and in a bid to escape she excused herself and headed towards the powder room.

Big mistake, she realised minutes later as Camille quickly joined her. A queue was inevitable, given the number of stalls, and Hannah stood stiffly as she waited for Camille to strike.

She wasn't disappointed. 'Don't imagine you can hide behind a bodyguard. I suppose you think you're very clever.'

Hannah turned slightly to look at the Frenchwoman. 'Not at all,' she responded lightly. 'And the bodyguard is there at Miguel's instigation.'

Camille's expression became an icy mask. 'Protecting his business investment.'

'Of course.' It was the truth, so why deny it?

'But there is a bonus,' Hannah continued quietly. 'I get to share his bed, his life, and bear his children.'

She took a shallow breath and released it. 'Admit you failed, Camille, and go look for another rich man who's not averse to your game-playing.' She paused fractionally. 'And take Luc with you.'

'He's a practised lover,' the Frenchwoman intimated with deliberate maliciousness.

'Do you think so?' Hannah contrived a slight frown. 'I found his foreplay technique reasonable, but his application needed work.' She managed a careless shrug. 'Maybe he's improved.'

Camille swung her hand in a vicious arc, except this time Hannah was prepared, and she took a quick sidestep so the slap didn't connect.

Hannah was aware of a few surprised gasps, then Renee was there, her normally composed features fierce with anger.

'You've said quite enough, Camille! Now get out of here at once. There is another set of facilities if you must use them.' She turned towards her daughter. 'Darling, are you all right?'

'Yes. Thanks,' she added, and couldn't help wondering if Miguel had sent Renee to her rescue.

'Come, let's go back to—'

'The table?' She shook her head. 'I really do need to freshen up. Tell Miguel I'll go straight to our seats.'

'I'll stay,' Renee said firmly.

'Then we'll have both our men sending out a

search party.' She could almost see the humour in the situation. 'Really, I'm fine.'

'Well,' her mother said doubtfully. 'If you're sure?'

A stall became vacant, and Hannah moved into it. Minutes later she paused in front of the long mirror to freshen her lipstick, then she emerged into the foyer.

She hadn't taken two steps when Miguel fell in beside her, and she shot him a steady look as he caught hold of her arm. 'First Renee, now *you*?'

'Another minute, and I'd have fetched you personally.'

'Entered a known *women's* domain? How brave.'

'Don't push it, *querida*,' he warned in sibilant anger.

They weren't moving in the direction of the auditorium. 'We're going the wrong way.'

'I'm taking you home.'

'The hell you are!' She resolutely refused to move. Her eyes sparked blue fire as she confronted him. 'I'm not missing the rest of the play.' She balled one hand into a fist and connected with his ribs. 'The only way you'll get me away from here is to toss me over your shoulder and carry me out!'

He was caught between laughter and voluble anger. 'Don't tempt me,' he bit back with a husky growl.

Hannah wrenched her arm from his grasp and marched, as well as four-inch stiletto heels would allow, towards the auditorium.

By the time she reached a set of double doors he

was beside her, and together they entered the dimmed theatre, located their seats, and slid into them.

Almost immediately the curtain rose and the next act commenced.

Hannah focused on the actors and their lines in a determined effort to forget Camille, Luc, and her inimitable husband. She succeeded, almost, rising from her seat with the audience to applaud the playwright, the cast, and the producer.

The exodus of patrons took a little while, and it was almost eleven when Miguel eased the Jaguar through the city streets. A shower of rain wet the bitumen, and she watched the automated swish of the windscreen wipers as the car turned into Toorak Road.

The headache that had niggled away at her temple for the past hour seemed to intensify, and as soon as he brought the car to a halt inside the garage she slid from her seat and preceded him into the house.

They reached the foyer, and his gaze sharpened as he took in her pale features. 'Take something for that headache, and go to bed.'

'Don't tell me what to do.'

'*Querida,*' Miguel drawled. 'You want to fight?'

'Yes, damn you!'

'There's a punch bag in the downstairs gym. Why don't you go try it out?'

He was amused, damn him. She threw him a dark glare. 'I might do that!'

'Just one thing,' he ventured indolently. 'Go and change first.'

She didn't even pause to think, she just bent one knee, pulled off a heeled shoe and threw it at him.

Miguel palmed it neatly, placed it carefully down onto a nearby side-table, and turned back towards her.

'Want to try again?'

This time it was her evening purse that flew through the air, and she cried out with rage as he scooped her into his arms and carried her upstairs.

Hannah hit out at his shoulders, his arms, anywhere she could connect, and groaned with angry frustration when she didn't seem to make any impression at all.

He reached the bedroom and entered it, kicking the door shut behind him, then he released her down onto the floor.

'Okay,' he growled huskily. 'That's enough.'

'Do you know how I feel?' she demanded vengefully.

'I'd say it's mutual.' He caught hold of her shoulders and held her still. 'Stop it.'

'Right at this moment, I think I hate you.'

'For being a target for some woman's warped mind?'

'I want to go to bed. Alone.' *Fool*, a tiny voice derided. You're taking your anger out on the wrong person. Except she wasn't being rational.

Miguel released her slowly. 'Then go to bed.' He turned and walked from the room, closing the door quietly behind him.

She looked at the door, and almost wished he'd slammed it. It would have made more sense.

Slowly she crossed to the window and looked out

over the darkened gardens. The moon was high, a large round white orb that cast a milky light onto the earth below, making long shadows of small shrubs, the trees, and duplicating the shape of the house. Somewhere in the distance a dog barked, and another joined it in a howling canine melody.

Hannah closed the curtains, then slowly undressed, removed her make-up, then she pulled on the silky slip she wore to bed and slid between the sheets, snapped off the bedside lamp, and lay staring into the darkness. Images filled her mind, prominent and intrusive, and her eyes swam until tears spilled and trickled slowly towards her ears, then dripped onto the pillow.

She brushed them away, twice, then determinedly closed her eyes in a bid to summon sleep.

Except she was still awake when Miguel entered the room a long time later. She heard him discard his clothes, and felt the faint depression of the mattress as he slid into bed.

Hold me, she silently begged him. Except the words wouldn't find voice, and she lay still, listening to his breathing steady and become slow and even in sleep. It would have been so easy to touch him. All she had to do was slide her hand until it encountered the warmth of his body.

Except she couldn't do it. Be honest, she silently castigated. You're afraid. Afraid that he might ignore the gesture or, worse, refuse it. And how would she feel if he did?

Shattered.

CHAPTER TEN

HANNAH woke to the sound of the shower running in the adjoining *en suite*, and she rolled over to check the digital clock. Seven.

She slid out of bed, gathered up fresh underwear, her robe, and adjourned to the next bedroom where she showered and changed.

It would have been easy to join Miguel, just pull open the glass door and step in beside him as she did every morning. Except today she couldn't, not after last night.

And whose fault was that? a silent voice taunted.

She drew a deep breath, then returned to their room to see Miguel in the process of dressing.

He cast her a long measured look, which she returned, then she discarded her nightwear onto the bed and crossed to her walk-in wardrobe to select something to wear.

'Do you intend sulking for long?' His voice was a slightly inflected drawl, which she ignored as she stepped into sheer black stockings, then selected one of three black suits she chose to wear to the boutique.

When she emerged, he was standing in her path, and she just looked at him.

'Hannah,' he warned silkily.

'I am *not* sulking!' She *never* sulked; it wasn't in her nature.

And I don't hate you, she added silently, unable to say the words aloud. Dear heaven, what had possessed her to say such a thing? Reaction, angry tension. But words, once said, were difficult to retract. Except the longer she left the anger to simmer, the harder it would be to explain.

'What do you want me to say?' Her eyes darkened and became stormy. 'I'm sorry I acted like a bitch last night? Okay, I apologise.'

'Apology accepted.'

Hannah looked at him sharply. 'Don't patronise me.'

'Stop it right there,' Miguel warned.

'I'm not a child, dammit!' What was she doing, for heaven's sake? She was like a runaway train that couldn't stop.

'Then don't behave like one.'

'You'll forgive me if I don't join you for breakfast,' Hannah said stiffly. 'I'll stop off at a café for coffee and a croissant.'

She moved past him and entered the *en suite*. She picked up the hairbrush and attacked her hair, stroking the brush through its length until her scalp tingled, then she applied minimum make-up.

Her eyes widened as she caught sight of Miguel via mirrored reflection as he moved in to stand behind her, and her fingers faltered and tightened around the tube of lipstick.

She felt like a finely tuned string that was about to

snap as he turned her round to face him, and she was powerless to move as his head descended.

'This, *this*,' Miguel breathed close to her mouth, 'is important. Nothing else.' And he kissed her, thoroughly, until her head spun. Then he released her, and walked from the room.

Hannah gripped hold of the marbled vanity unit and tried to regain her breath. Dear heaven, what was the matter with her?

She had no idea how long she stood there, only that it seemed an age before she gathered up her bag, slid her feet into heeled shoes, and made her way downstairs to the garage.

Ten minutes later she parked the Porsche, then crossed the road, bought a daily newspaper, entered a coffee bar and joined the patrons enjoying breakfast.

At nine she unlocked the boutique and spent the next half-hour on the phone chasing a courier who had been supposed to deliver late the previous afternoon, and hadn't.

The morning dragged, and trying to continually pin a smile on her face began to take its toll. How could she pretend to be happy when inside she was breaking into a thousand pieces?

'Are you ill?' Elaine enquired with concern at midday.

'No.'

An inquisitive smile curved her attractive mouth. 'Pregnant?'

'No.'

'You sound hesitant,' Elaine teased. 'Could that be a maybe, but it's too soon to tell?'

Hannah simply shook her head. 'Go take your lunch break.' She extracted her purse and took out a note. 'Can you bring me back a chicken and salad sandwich and bottled water?' Today she'd eat in the small back room instead of spending her usual half-hour break at a nearby café.

Elaine finished at four, and the afternoon seemed to drag as Hannah checked her stock list, then made a few phone calls. A fax came through alerting that a special order would be despatched by overnight courier, and she made a note to phone the client.

Miguel's forceful image haunted her, as it had all morning, only now it was worse, for there was no one to talk to, no client entering the boutique to attract her attention, and the phone didn't ring.

Thinking about last night made her stomach twist into a painful knot. Somehow Miguel's controlled anger had been worse than if he'd let fly a string of pithy oaths, or thrown something, yelled at her. Instead he'd reduced her angry outburst to a childish tantrum, and that irked and angered her more than she wanted to admit.

The electronic buzzer sounded, alerting her to someone entering the boutique, and she summoned a warm smile as she moved out from behind the desk.

'Hannah, darling.'

'Mother.' Renee always rang before calling in. Always. The fact she hadn't this time caused Hannah's forehead to crease into a slight frown.

'I know, I should have phoned first. But I was close by…' She trailed off, before launching into an explanation, 'Lunch with an old friend, darling. And I thought I'd just pop in and say hello.'

'It's great to see you.' She injected enthusiasm into her voice and crossed the floor to bestow the customary air-kiss to each cheek. 'The scarves arrived this morning. I put a few aside that I thought you might like. Would you like to see them?'

Business. If she could keep everything on a business footing, maybe Renee wouldn't notice the fine cracks in her daughter's façade.

'Oh, please, darling.'

Hannah retrieved the box, extracted three scarves and spread them across the counter. They were pure silk, exquisitely patterned, and an attractive fashion accessory.

Renee selected two, then crossed to the blouse rack, chose one, then moved to the desk. 'I'll take these, darling.' She gave a soft exclamation, and followed it with a ladylike curse. 'I don't believe it. I've left my bag in the car.'

'Locked, I hope,' Hannah said at once, concern marring her features.

'Of course, locked, darling. I have my keys.' She held them up in plain sight. 'I remember activating the alarm.'

'Where are you parked?'

'This side of the street, just a few cars down.' She held out the keys. 'Would you mind fetching it for me?' She cast the empty boutique a cursory glance. 'It'll only take a minute.'

Maybe a breath of fresh air might lift her mood, Hannah determined as she accepted the keys and made for the door.

It was hot outside, the sun's brightness intense after the air-conditioned coolness indoors. A few cars down meant she met the worst of the glare as she walked towards her mother's car, and she lifted a hand to shade her eyes. Only to come to a dead halt at the sight of a familiar tall frame standing beside Renee's Lexus.

Miguel. Looking totally relaxed and at ease, his expression shaded behind dark sunglasses. A deceptive pose, for she had no doubt beneath that calm exterior lay the coiled strength of a predator.

There was a part of her that wanted to turn back and return to the boutique, where her mother's presence would ensure civility was maintained. Yet she refused to take the easy way out. Whatever they needed to say to each other had to be said.

Miguel saw the moment she mentally squared her shoulders, witnessed the slight lift of her chin, and accurately defined the expression in her clear blue eyes.

It was her nature to confront, resolve, and move forward. He was bargaining on her doing just that.

'It's four thirty,' Hannah said evenly as she took the necessary steps to reach the Lexus. 'What are you doing here?'

He pulled back the cuff of his jacket, checked his

watch, then trapped her gaze. 'A few minutes past that, if you want total accuracy.'

Miguel didn't shift position, and she was forced to move in close as she deactivated the alarm, unlocked the passenger door, retrieved her mother's bag, then reversed the security process.

'Shall we return Renee's bag?' he queried mildly, and she threw him a measured look.

'We?'

He caught hold of her elbow, firming his grasp as she made to wrench away. *'We,'* he reiterated firmly.

'Miguel—'

'There's the easy way where we walk back to the boutique. Or I can hoist you over one shoulder and carry you. Which would you prefer?'

Her eyes sparked angry fire. 'You're giving me a choice?'

He brushed his thumb over the generous curve of her mouth. 'No.'

Her palms itched with the urge to slap him.

'Don't.' The warning was silky soft and curled round her nerve-ends.

Without a word she turned and made her way back to the boutique, aware of an explosive electric force field that surrounded them.

Hannah was startlingly aware of him, his proximity, the faint aroma of his aftershave, the clean smell of his clothes. His grasp on her elbow would tighten in a heartbeat if she attempted to pull free.

Four shop fronts, a matter of mere metres, and they reached the boutique. She didn't even question his intention to enter, for it was clearly evident he meant to.

She paused, her features strained, her eyes too dark. 'Is there a purpose to this?'

'Yes.'

Hannah extended her hand to open the door, only to have it swing inward.

'Ah, there you are,' Renee declared, her features carefully schooled. 'There was one phone call, which I dealt with.'

Hannah looked from one to the other, and settled on Miguel, suspicion uppermost. 'You set this up.' She turned towards her mother. 'Didn't you?'

'Guilty.'

'*Why?*' Hannah demanded, sorely tried.

'Go get your bag,' Miguel instructed. 'We're leaving.'

'I'll stay and close the boutique,' Renee informed before her daughter had a chance to protest.

'No.' Hannah threw Miguel a vengeful glare. 'And if you try any macho tactics, I'll call the police.'

'Call them.' It took two seconds to sweep an arm beneath her knees and lift her against his chest.

Renee crossed quickly to the desk, opened a cupboard, retrieved Hannah's bag, and handed it to Miguel.

'I'll never forgive you for this,' Hannah vented as she closed her fingers into a fist and set a bruising punch to his shoulder.

He turned and walked out the door, traversed the

pavement to where his car was parked, unlocked the door, then he thrust her into the passenger seat.

The next instant he crossed round to the driver's side, then slid in behind the wheel.

The engine fired and settled into a soft purr as he eased the car out of its parking space and into the flow of traffic along Toorak Road.

Hannah didn't trust herself to speak. There was too much anger to bother with meaningless words.

Instead, she looked beyond the windscreen, noting the traffic, people walking, children, mothers laughing, scolding. Movement, life. Outside, the world continued to evolve, along with people's lives.

From inside, somehow it didn't seem real. She might as well have been viewing the scene on television.

Familiar streets, familiar locale. She passed by here five days out of seven.

But not quite this far, she suddenly realised.

'You've missed the turn.'

'We're not going home.' Miguel's voice was a faintly inflected drawl, and she looked at him carefully, seeing the strength and sense of purpose evident.

'Perhaps you'd care to enlighten me exactly where we *are* going?'

He slanted her a quick glance. 'Wait and see.'

'Oh, for heaven's sake,' Hannah dismissed angrily, and refrained from offering so much as another word.

The flow of traffic intensified as they neared the city, and she contained her surprise as Miguel swung the car into the entrance of one of the inner city's most exclusive hotels.

The porter opened her door, leaving her little recourse but to slip out from the passenger seat.

What on earth were they doing here? In a hotel, for God's sake, when they had a beautiful luxurious home less than fifteen minutes distant? It was crazy. Even more puzzling was the fact Miguel had apparently checked in, for he led the way to the bank of lifts adjacent the foyer.

Hannah spared him a level glance as they rode the lift to a high floor, and within minutes Miguel ushered her into a spacious, elegantly appointed suite.

She crossed to the wide plate-glass window and parted the filmy day curtains to look at the view, then she slowly turned back to face him.

He had removed his jacket, and was in the process of loosening his tie.

'You owe me an explanation.'

Miguel discarded the tie, undid the top few buttons of his shirt, removed cuff-links from each sleeve, then he crossed to the bar-fridge.

'What would you like to drink?'

She was angry and on edge. 'Stop playing the gentleman.'

He paused, and she had the impression of harnessed strength and immeasurable control. For some reason it made her feel apprehensive.

His eyes held an expression she didn't care to define. 'What would you have me play, *amante*?'

She was reminded of silk being razed by steel, and

she crossed her arms, hugging them against her mid-riff in a unconscious protective gesture.

'The savage?' he posed. 'A husband who is moved to such anger, it is all he can do not to strangle his beautiful wife's neck?' He extracted bottled water, unscrewed the cap, filled a glass and handed it to her, then he took out a can of cola, pulled the tab, and drained some of the contents.

'Or perhaps I should beat you.' He lifted the can and took a long swallow. 'Believe I am sorely tempted to do both.'

'Try it,' Hannah said tightly.

He cast her a long dark look that sent shivers scudding down the length of her spine. 'Don't push me.'

Without thinking she threw the contents of her glass in his face, watching with a sense of mesmerised disbelief as the cold water splashed from his broad features down onto his shirt, leaving a huge wet patch that was impossible to ignore.

She didn't move, despite a terrible sense of panic that urged her to run as far and as fast as she could.

Instead, she stood glaring at him in silent defiance.

His eyes didn't leave hers as he set the can aside, then in seeming slow motion he pulled the shirt free from his trousers, undid the buttons, then he shrugged it off and draped it over a nearby chair before turning to face her.

With deliberate movements he reached for a neatly folded towel displayed in plain sight and removed the excess moisture from his face, then he tossed the towel onto the bed.

He was an impressive sight. Olive skin stretched over hard musculature, the liberal sprinkle of dark hair at his chest, a tight stomach, firm waist, with not a spare ounce of flesh in evidence.

'Are you done?'

'It depends.'

He took a step towards her, and she stood her ground.

'So brave,' Miguel mocked silkily, watching her pupils dilate as he drew close.

She was damned if she'd beg, and the single word emerged as a warning. 'Don't.'

He didn't touch her. 'Don't—*what*, specifically?'

'I'll fight you,' she said fiercely, unaware that her hands had tightened into fists, or that her stance had altered slightly preparatory for attack.

'You can't win.'

'I can try.' She would, too. Self defence was an art form she'd studied to a degree, and she had the element of surprise on her side.

He saw the slight lift of her chin, the muscle flex at the edge of her jaw, the anger, the fire so close to the surface.

'Do you want to so badly?'

'*Yes,*' Hannah vented, and saw him slide a hand into each trouser pocket.

'Then go ahead.'

Hit him? For all the times she'd wanted to, for the few occasions she actually had...now that he was placing himself at her mercy, she found she couldn't do it.

Miguel caught each fleeting expression on her mobile features, and accurately defined every one of them.

'I guess we need to talk,' she offered slowly.

'We did that. It didn't resolve anything.'

Her face paled as she recalled the explosive scene they'd shared early this morning.

'Miguel—'

Whatever else she might have said remained locked in her throat as his mouth slanted down to cover hers in a kiss that tore at the very roots of her emotional foundation.

There was nothing punishing about it, just intense evocative passion that seemed to plunder the depths of her soul, dragging something from her she was reluctant to give.

She didn't *want* to respond. Dear heaven, how could she, when there was so much hurt and anguish?

It was almost as if he was trying to tap into her fragile heart, to instil something so infinitely precious that meant more, so much more than mere words could convey.

His mouth was the only part of his body touching her. He could easily have drawn her into his arms, used his hands to mould her slender frame to his, his heavy arousal in evidence. Employed sensual body heat to tantalise her senses, to touch and tease with such skilful expertise she would soon shatter into a thousand pieces. *His*.

Yet he did none of those things. There was just his

mouth, and the mesmeric intoxication of heat and passion.

She hated the distance between them, and it took tremendous strength of will not to sink into him. *This*, after all, was the one level of communication at which they excelled.

Sex. Really great sex.

She'd thought it was enough. She'd even managed to convince herself that *love* didn't matter. But it did, and a little part of her had slowly died with each passing day.

Sensation flared, spiralling through her body, filling it with a sweet sorcery only Miguel had the power to wield.

A faint sob rose and died in her throat, a slight compulsive movement he felt rather than heard, and he sensed the way her hands rose, then fell again as she sought control.

The long slow sweep of his tongue against her own almost caused her to lose it, and she began to shake beneath the emotional weight of resisting him.

He sensed the moment she ignored her mind and went with her heart, felt the first tentative touch of her hands as they crept to his shoulders and twined together round his neck.

Something within him convulsed, and a deep shudder raked his powerful frame as he drew her close in against him.

His kiss deepened, possessing with shameless hunger as he led her down a path towards sensual conflagration.

Hannah lost track of time and a sense of place in the need to be part of him. The rest of his clothes, hers, were an unwanted intrusion, and her fingers sought the buckle fastening the belt on his trousers, only to have him shift slightly and cover her hand with his own before gently placing her at arm's length.

Her eyes widened and seemed too large in her face. Uncertain, she edged the tip of her tongue along the swollen curve of her lip. The gesture was unbidden, and she saw his eyes flare, then become incredibly dark.

He placed a finger over her lips, felt the faint tremble, and cupped her jaw.

'You are my life,' Miguel said gently. '*Amada*, the very air that I breathe. Everything.' A finger traced the pulsing cord to the base of her throat and settled in the sensitive hollow above the rapid beat of her pulse. 'You have my heart, all that I am.' His smile held a warmth that made her breath hitch. 'Always.'

Hannah wasn't capable of uttering a word.

'From the beginning,' he added. 'I took one look, and there could be no one else. Only *you*.'

She found her voice with difficulty. 'But we—'

'Married to please our respective parents, ensure the business *stayed in the family*?' He brushed a thumb along the curve of her lower lip. 'Do you really believe that?'

Her mouth quivered. 'You said—'

'I asked you to marry me.'

'I thought—'

'You think too much,' Miguel chastised gently. 'I love you. *You*,' he emphasised. 'For everything you are.'

'You loved me?' she queried as hope began to unfurl. 'From the beginning?'

'Do you really believe I'm the kind of man who would tie himself legally to a woman, contemplate making her the mother of my children—' He broke off, and shook his head. '*Querida*, haven't you come to know me better than that?'

Yes, she had. Or, at least, she'd thought she had before Camille had begun playing her games.

'Camille—'

'I barely refrained from strangling her. As to Luc—' A muscle tensed at the edge of his jaw, and his eyes took on a dangerous gleam. 'The temptation to break his jaw was never far from my mind.'

Something that had been evident on occasion, Hannah reflected. Although at the time she'd thought Miguel was simply playing the part expected of him.

And Camille?

'Notice that an interim apprehended violence order would be filed against Camille was issued yesterday. I understand she chose to take the option of dropped charges if she remove herself from the state and the country within twenty-four hours,' Miguel informed her, reading her mind.

His words were so clipped and hard, Hannah didn't doubt *he* had delivered the ultimatum in a manner Camille couldn't fail to understand.

'I see,' she said slowly.

One eyebrow slanted with musing humour. 'What do you see, *amante*?'

She lifted a hand, then let it fall to her side.

'Where do we go from here?'

'Now?' Miguel pulled her gently back into his arms, and nuzzled the delicate curve at the base of her neck. 'I'm going to make love with my wife.' He drew the soft skin into his mouth and grazed it with his teeth.

A tremor shook her slender frame as liquid fire flooded her veins, heating her body to fever pitch.

'Show her how infinitely precious she is to me.' Slowly and with infinite care, he freed the buttons on her blouse, then slid it from her arms and discarded it. Next came the zip fastening on her skirt, and he skimmed slip and briefs over her hips in one easy movement. Hannah stepped out of her heeled shoes as he unfastened the clip of her bra.

'And ensure she never has reason to doubt my love for her.' He traced the curve of one breast, then brushed his fingers back and forth across a rosy peak, watching as the bud protruded before lowering his head to capture it in his mouth.

Her body arched as he suckled, and a gasp emerged from her throat when he rolled the tender bud with the edge of his teeth, leaving her teetering on the brink between pleasure and pain.

'This isn't fair,' she inclined, reaching for the buckle on his trousers, then the zip, and seconds later he kicked aside his trousers and briefs.

'Better?'

'Much.'

'I intended to take you to dinner,' Miguel informed her as she began a subtle exploration that soon promised to have dangerous consequences.

'Maybe later.'

'With champagne,' he added for good measure, then drew in a deep breath and held it as she enclosed him.

'Room service,' Hannah offered an instant before he carried her down onto the bed.

CHAPTER ELEVEN

THEY did eat, well after the witching hour of midnight.

The lovemaking had been hard and fast, then afterwards they'd indulged themselves with a sensual feast that surpassed anything they'd previously shared. Vibrant, erotic, it was sensual magic at its most primitive.

Following a leisurely shower they donned courtesy robes, and sipped fine French champagne while they waited for room service.

When they finished the food, she leaned back in her chair. There were questions she wanted to ask. Words she needed to say. *Now*, a tiny voice prompted. Say them now.

There were tiny lines fanning out from the corners of his eyes, and his features showed evidence of emerging dark stubble.

She looked at him carefully, seeing the strength, the aura of power he projected, and knew that it would always be there. For her.

'I love you,' she revealed with quiet sincerity, and saw his features soften.

His eyes were dark, so very dark, their expression unguarded so as to almost make her catch her breath at the wealth of emotion evident. *'Gracias, mi mujer,'* he acknowledged gently.

'I always have. If I hadn't,' Hannah assured him, 'I would never have agreed to marry you.' She swallowed a small lump that suddenly rose in her throat. 'You're everything I need. All I could ever want.' Her eyes became luminous with shimmering tears. 'My life.'

Was it possible for a heart to stop beating? That emotion could be so intense it could cut off the ability to speak?

Miguel stood and pulled her into his arms. His mouth was an erotic instrument as he kissed her, gently at first, then with increasing passion.

Hannah became lost, adrift in a sea of emotion and she simply held onto his shoulders as she met and matched his fervour.

How long did they stand there, locked in each other's arms? She had no recollection of time.

Slowly he eased his mouth from hers, pressing soft kisses to her swollen lips as she sighed in protest, and she groaned a little when he disengaged her arms and crossed the room.

She watched idly as he extracted something from his jacket pocket, and returned to press a slim jeweller's case into her hand.

'I have something for you.'

'Miguel—'

'Open it.'

She did so, carefully, and felt the sudden prick of tears. Nestled in a bed of velvet was an exquisite drop necklace and matching earrings. Beautifully delicate, it linked Argyle pink and white diamonds alternately with a pear-shaped pink diamond at the base of the drop.

'They're beautiful,' Hannah whispered, feeling the moisture well, then spill to run down each cheek in a slow rivulet that paused momentarily at the edge of her jaw. 'Thank you.'

'Tears, Hannah?'

At his teasing query she blinked them away, and brushed shaky fingers across each cheek. 'I can't seem to stop.'

Miguel removed the necklace, placed it in position and fastened the safety clip. Then he leant down and brushed his lips to her temple.

The intricate centre star-burst lay just beneath the hollow of her throat, with its single line of pink sapphires and diamonds dropping several inches towards the soft swell of her breasts.

The fact he had remembered was one thing. Since the description had been her own and didn't refer to anything she'd seen, it meant he'd consigned a jeweller to craft it to this specific design.

'Don't you want to see how it looks?'

Hannah shook her head. 'It's the most beautiful thing I've ever owned,' she said softly. 'Special,' she added, aware he knew just how much the gift meant to her.

She reached for the clasp, only to have him still her hands.

'Leave it on.'

Without a further word she drew his head down to hers and initiated a kiss that proved so evocative it could have only one ending.

Later, much later, Miguel curved her in against him and pressed a light kiss to her temple. 'Sleep, *amante*. Tomorrow is another day.'

Hannah woke to the peal of the doorbell, and Miguel ushered in the waiter delivering room-service breakfast.

What time was it? She cast a hurried glance at the digital clock on the bedside pedestal, and gave a groan.

Eight-fifteen! Dear heaven, she was due to open the boutique at nine, and she needed to shower, dress, get home and collect a fresh change of clothes...

With rapid movements she thrust aside the covers and slid to her feet. The shower...

'*Amada*, slow down,' Miguel growled in husky chastisement, and she cast him a harried glance.

'The boutique— You should have woken me...'

'Come and have breakfast.' He sounded indolently amused. 'You're not going anywhere.'

'What do you mean I'm not going anywhere? It's late—'

His dark musing expression held warm appreciation of her nudity, and she quickly caught up a robe, thrust her arms through the sleeves and hurriedly caught the silk edges together.

He extended a hand, caught hold of hers, and pulled her close.

'Miguel,' she protested in exasperation. 'We don't have time—'

'Yes, we do.'

'No, we don't.' She dragged fingers through the tousled length of her hair, and made an effort to free her hand.

Except she didn't stand a chance as his mouth covered hers in a lingering kiss that almost destroyed the will to move. Almost. It was she who pulled away first, and only, she suspected, because he allowed it.

He could, he knew, slide the silk from her shoulders and pull her down onto the bed. Early morning lovemaking was a mutual indulgence that made for a great start to the day. Today, however, it would have to wait.

'Renee will open the boutique this morning.'

She stilled, and gave him a searching look. 'Why?'

Miguel led her towards the table where the waiter had laid out their breakfast. 'Sit down and we'll eat.'

'I'm not doing a thing until you tell me what's going on.'

'Okay,' Miguel said easily. 'We're due to board an international flight in a few hours.'

She stilled, and her eyes were wide as she looked at him. 'What did you say?'

He reached out an arm and drew her forward and into a chair, then he took the seat opposite. 'You heard.'

'How?'

He cast her a musing glance. 'The usual way, I imagine.'

'I mean, how can we get away at such short notice?'

'Delegate.'

'I can't—'

'Yes, you can.' He drank half of his orange juice in one long swallow. 'Cindy returns to work on Monday, she will manage the boutique with Elaine's help, and Renee will go in at four each afternoon to close.'

'But—'

'The world as we know it won't end if we take time out,' Miguel relayed quietly.

He was right, it wouldn't. It was just so...*sudden*. So unexpected.

Hannah took a sip of orange juice, then another. 'Where are we going?'

'Hawaii.'

Oh, my, did he possess some kind of mind-reading gift? She mentally pictured white sand, blue sea, and white-crested surf, sunshine, and tranquillity. Lazy days, long, languid nights. Heaven.

She almost dared not ask. 'How long?'

'A week in Honolulu, and a week on Maui.'

'Honolulu?' she queried, a slow, sweet smile curving her lips. Maui. She didn't know which held the most appeal. 'Really?' Her eyes acquired a gleam. *'Today?'*

His mouth twitched with wry amusement. 'Don't look at me like that. Or we won't get out of this suite, let alone catch a scheduled flight.'

Hannah laughed, a light-hearted sound that stole round his heart and tugged a little. 'You think so?'

He reached out a hand and placed a finger over her lips. 'Breakfast, *querida*.'

'Okay,' she acquiesced. She held up one hand and began counting off her fingers. 'Hmm. A nine-hour flight.' Her eyes acquired a devilish sparkle. 'That gives me plenty of time to plan exactly how I intend to reward you.'

'Minx,' he said, tempted to discard breakfast altogether.

'Pity we need to go home to pack.'

'No,' Miguel discounted. 'We don't. I have our bags in the boot of the car.'

She couldn't restrain an incredulous smile. '*You* packed for me?'

'I have as much as you need,' he said with musing solemnity. 'Anything else you can buy there. Besides,' he added indolently, 'I don't plan on having you wear much at all most of the time.'

Hannah leaned across the table and pressed a finger to his lips. 'Well, I have news for you, *amante*. I plan to swim, lie in the sun, go for long walks, and read. And a pleasant meal among fellow diners is also a prerequisite.' Her eyes sparkled and acquired the hue of brilliant blue topaz. 'If you've only tossed briefs and a robe into my bag, you're in serious trouble.'

'Try…an evening suit, a dress or two, shorts, a few tops, bikini, shoes…' Miguel trailed off, then opened his mouth and playfully nipped her finger with the edge of his teeth before releasing it.

'*Food,*' she mocked gently, and began doing justice to cereal and fruit, following it with toast and strong black coffee.

They made the flight with only minutes to spare, and Hannah divided her attention between the pages of a spellbinding murder mystery and the movies offered on-screen.

It was late when they landed in Honolulu, and almost midnight by the time they checked into their hotel.

The luxury suite on a high floor overlooking Waikiki beach was superb, and Hannah crossed to the wide expanse of plate glass and slid open doors onto the lanai.

A gentle breeze wafted in from the ocean, and the air held the fresh smell of the sea. Twinkling lights outlined the mainland arching towards Diamond Head.

Miguel moved in close behind her and linked his arms around her waist. His chin rested on top of her head as she leaned back against him.

'It's magical,' she murmured softly. Melbourne, home, *Camille*, seemed so far away. Like a bad dream from which she'd just awoken. 'Thank you.'

'For what, precisely?'

'Bringing me here,' she said simply. Taking affirmative action, believing in me...*us*, she added silently.

Miguel's hands tightened fractionally, and he lowered his head to savour the vulnerable hollow at the base of her neck. 'My pleasure.'

'I've reached a decision,' Hannah said slowly, feeling the heat slipping through her body at his touch. It was like an aphrodisiac, powerful, potent, and electric. She felt malleable, *his*. 'If you approve.'

'Are you asking, or telling me?' he teased, aware of her quickening heartbeat, the way her body was poised between want and surrender.

'I thought—' She paused, and dragged in a quick breath as his hand cupped her breast and began caressing its vulnerable peak.

'Hmm?' he queried musingly. 'What did you think, *querida*?'

'After Christmas might be a good time to promote Cindy.'

'A sensible decision.'

'I think I'll keep Elaine on part-time, just to help out.'

'I assume this is leading somewhere?' Miguel prompted leisurely.

'Babies,' Hannah ventured with a soft smile. 'How do you feel about starting our own family?'

He felt as if someone had punched him in the solar plexus. A child? His mind leapt ahead to a blonde angel the mirror image of her mother. Maybe a dark-haired son who would drive his mother mad with boyish pranks... *Por Dios*, Hannah heavy with child, the birth... He went pale at the thought of her in pain.

'Are you sure about this?'

She twisted in his arms as she turned to face him. 'You're not?' She searched his features in the half-light, and glimpsed something evident she couldn't define.

'I can't think of anything more special, other than you, that you could gift me,' Miguel declared fervently.

Hannah felt the slight tremor that ran through his large body, and she wound her arms round his waist and pulled him close.

'Maybe we should go inside,' she teased lightly, 'and practise a little.' A warm chuckle emerged from her throat. 'Besides, I have a particular reward to bestow.'

Together they re-entered the suite, closed the door to the lanai, then drew the curtains.

Their own private world, Hannah mused as she removed her outer clothes and entered the shower. Miguel joined her, and they took their time, enjoying the promise, the anticipation of the loving they would always share.

During the following few days they delighted in playing tourist. They rode the tramcar, hired a limousine for the day and toured the island.

Midweek they took a flight out to Maui, and spent a wonderfully relaxing six days in a hotel right on the beach overlooking the ocean. Lovely sunny days walking on the beach, lazing beneath the spread of palm trees reading, listening to music on the Walkman. They swam in the ocean, frequented the hotel pool, played tennis, then dined in one of several restaurants, before retiring to their suite to make long, sweet love through the night.

Miguel rose early in the morning to use the laptop for an hour, and checked his cell-phone before they went to dinner each evening as a brief concession to the outside business world.

Hannah didn't mind. It was enough they were together in a wonderfully idyllic part of the world.

On their return to Honolulu they shopped in several exclusive boutiques. 'Retail therapy,' Hannah teased as she added yet another brightly coloured designer bag to the few Miguel indulgently carried in each hand.

There were gifts to select for Renee, Carlo and Esteban, as well as something for Cindy and Elaine.

In one shop she caught sight of the most exquisite little dress for a baby girl, and bought it with Elise in mind.

'Are you done?' Miguel queried musingly as she emerged from yet another boutique.

'Not quite.' She had something very special in mind. 'I don't suppose you'll take those packages back to the hotel and give me an hour to shop alone?'

'Not a chance.'

'Okay,' Hannah said with resignation. 'But there are conditions.'

His eyes gleamed and his mouth moved to form a generous smile. 'And what would those be, *querida*?'

She sent him a sparkling glance as she lifted a hand and began ticking off each finger in turn. 'You won't question which shop I enter. You'll remain outside and won't look through the window. And under no circumstances will you come inside.'

He tilted his head slightly and regarded her thoughtfully. 'Bar there being a robbery, or some strange man attempts to chat you up.'

'Hmm,' she conceded, sending him an impish grin. 'That sounds fair.'

She looked no more than sixteen, Miguel ruminated musingly. Her hair was caught together at her nape, sunglasses rested atop her head, her make-up was minimal, her skin glowed a soft honey gold, and, attired in casual linen shorts and a singlet top, she didn't resemble anyone's wife.

Except she was his. The light of his life, his reason for living. It was something he gave grateful thanks to the good *Dios* for every day. He hadn't thought it possible to give up your life for another human being. But he'd give up his, for her, in a nanosecond.

Hannah paused outside an exclusive jewellery store, and turned towards him, her expression serious.

'Remember, you promised?'

'Go, *amante*.'

She did, earning circumspect interest from two male staff until she explained what she wanted, indicated a price range, and had their interest immediately switch to respect.

It took a while to make her selection. It took even longer to persuade them to have one of their craftsman engrave an inscription. A huge tip helped.

She had it placed in a beautiful velvet-lined box, gift-wrapped, charged to her own personal credit card, and she emerged through the glass doors with a satisfied smile.

It was their last evening in this beautiful paradise, and they'd dined at an exclusive restaurant in Honolulu's 'Pink Palace'. The food was delicious, the champagne superb, and the view out over the darkened ocean provided a peaceful backdrop.

Together they lingered, each reluctant to bring the evening to a close. For soon they'd have to return to their suite, call the porter to take their bags down to Reception, from where a cab would deliver them to the airport in order to catch the midnight flight home.

The waiter served coffee, and while Miguel signed the credit slip Hannah retrieved the gift-wrapped case from her bag and placed it on the table.

'For you,' she said gently as the waiter disappeared, and Miguel regarded her carefully for several seconds before reaching for the package.

He undid the gold ribbon, broke the seal, removed the wrapping, and opened the case.

Inside nestled in a bed of velvet lay a beautiful gold fob-watch with an attached chain.

'Hannah—'

'There's an inscription. Read it,' she encouraged, watching as he removed the watch and turned it over to read what had been engraved on the back.

Miguel, my heart, my soul. Hannah.

'*Dios,*' he breathed, momentarily speechless.

'There's a place inside for a photo,' she relayed softly. One that would change from year to year as they added to their family.

'*Gracias, amada.*' He rose to his feet and crossed round to kiss her.

Very thoroughly, Hannah mused long seconds later.

Together they left the table and made their way back to their suite.

A long flight lay ahead, and there was little time to spare.

'One lifetime won't be enough,' Miguel said gently as he drew her into his arms.

'Not nearly enough,' Hannah whispered an instant before she pulled his head down to hers.

The insistent peal of the telephone caused them to reluctantly draw apart, and Miguel picked up the handset, listened, then added a brief few words.

'The porter is on his way up, and the cab is waiting downstairs,' he relayed with something akin to regret, and her mouth curved into a warm smile.

'We'll be home tomorrow.'

His answering smile held a certain musing wryness.

'That's no help at all.'

A soft laugh emerged from her lips. 'Patience, *querido*, is good for the soul.'

He bent his head and kissed her with such gentle evocativeness, she wanted to cry. 'I'll remind you of that, later.'

They had the rest of their lives, and together they would make each day count. For ever.

EPILOGUE

ALEXINA KATHLYN SANTANAS was born eleven months, three weeks and four days later. A joy to her mother, and cherished with idolatry awe by her father.

Family and close friends attended the christening and returned to Miguel and Hannah's Toorak home to offer congratulations and toast the blonde-haired angel's health and future happiness.

The sun shone brightly that day, and there was much laughter as everyone celebrated the event.

The guests departed early evening, and it was almost nine when Hannah retreated to the nursery to feed her daughter.

It had been a magical day, Hannah reflected as she changed Alexina and prepared to put her to the breast. She was a placid child, except at moments when she required sustenance or needed changing. Now, she was hungry, and her tiny fists beat an agitated dance before she latched on to suckle strongly.

Hannah looked at the perfect tiny features, the fine textured skin, and felt her heart swell with maternal pride. She really was the sweetest little thing. A precious gift.

What a difference a year made, she decided dreamily. Together she and Miguel had travelled to Rome, toured Italy and spent time in Andalusia. Cindy now ran the Toorak boutique with Elaine's help.

Life, she decided, was very sweet.

'How is she?'

Hannah had been so rapt in her own thoughts she hadn't noticed Miguel had quietly entered the room. She lifted her head and gave him the sort of smile that took hold of his heart and made it beat a whole lot faster.

Did she know how much he loved her? Couldn't fail to, he mused silently as he crossed to her side and stood watching while she disengaged their daughter and handed her to him to burp.

Minutes later he laid Alexina down carefully in her cot, drew the covers, then enfolded Hannah close to his side as they stood watching their daughter sleep.

'She's beautiful,' Miguel said softly. 'Just like her mother.' He turned as Hannah leant her head against his chest, and brushed his lips to her forehead. 'Time for us, *querida*.'

'Mmm,' she responded witchingly. 'Sounds interesting.' She lifted her head to look at him. 'What do you have in mind?'

He adjusted the baby monitor, then led her into their bedroom. 'Pleasuring you.'

'Isn't that a bit one-sided?'

He slowly undid the buttons on her top, and freed the rest of her clothes. His mouth slanted down to capture hers, and she kissed him back, swept away by the tide of passion as he gently pressed her down onto the bed.

'Later,' Miguel murmured. 'You get to have your turn.'

She did, although not for long. A thin reedy cry came through the baby monitor, and she stilled, waiting for another to follow it. When it did, she pressed a light kiss to her husband's thigh, then slid from the bed.

'Our daughter has no sense of timing,' Miguel groaned huskily as Hannah pulled on a robe.

'I'll be back,' she promised, and she was, several minutes later after soothing Alexina to sleep.

'Wind,' she enlightened succinctly as she slipped into bed and reached for him. 'Now, where were we?'

'I would say,' Miguel evinced huskily, 'just about there.' His breath caught, then hissed between his teeth as she caressed an acutely sensitive part of his male appendage.

It didn't take long for him to break, and Hannah exulted in the way he took control, entering her in one long thrust that soon settled into a rhythm as old as time.

A shimmering sensual feast shared by two people who loved to the depths of their souls. Without reason, other than they were twin halves of a whole. Beyond mortal life, for all eternity.

Harlequin truly does make any time special. . . . This year we are celebrating weddings in style!

To help us celebrate, we want you to tell us how wearing the Harlequin wedding gown will make your wedding day special. As the grand prize, Harlequin will offer one lucky bride the chance to **"Walk Down the Aisle"** in the Harlequin wedding gown!

There's more...

For her honeymoon, she and her groom will spend five nights at the **Hyatt Regency Maui.** As part of this five-night honeymoon at the hotel renowned for its romantic attractions, the couple will enjoy a candlelit dinner for two in Swan Court, a sunset sail on the hotel's catamaran, and duet spa treatments.

A HYATT RESORT AND SPA   Maui ▪ Molokai ▪ Lanai

To enter, please write, in, 250 words or less, how wearing the Harlequin wedding gown will make your wedding day special. The entry will be judged based on its emotionally compelling nature, its originality and creativity, and its sincerity. This contest is open to Canadian and U.S. residents only and to those who are 18 years of age and older. There is no purchase necessary to enter. Void where prohibited. See further contest rules attached. Please send your entry to:

Walk Down the Aisle Contest

In Canada	In U.S.A.
P.O. Box 637	P.O. Box 9076
Fort Erie, Ontario	3010 Walden Ave.
L2A 5X3	Buffalo, NY. 14269-9076

You can also enter by visiting www.eHarlequin.com
Win the Harlequin wedding gown and the vacation of a lifetime!
The deadline for entries is October 1, 2001.

HARLEQUIN®
Makes any time special ®

PHWDACONT1

HARLEQUIN WALK DOWN THE AISLE TO MAUI CONTEST 1197
OFFICIAL RULES
NO PURCHASE NECESSARY TO ENTER

1. To enter, follow directions published in the offer to which you are responding. Contest begins April 2, 2001, and ends on October 1, 2001. Method of entry may vary. Mailed entries must be postmarked by October 1, 2001, and received by October 8, 2001.

2. Contest entry may be, at times, presented via the Internet, but will be restricted solely to residents of certain geographic areas that are disclosed on the Web site. To enter via the Internet, if permissible, access the Harlequin Web site (www.eHarlequin.com) and follow the directions displayed online. Online entries must be received by 11:59 p.m. E.S.T. on October 1, 2001.

   In lieu of submitting an entry online, enter by mail by hand-printing (or typing) on an 8½" x 11" plain piece of paper, your name, address (including zip code), Contest number/name and in 250 words or fewer, why winning a Harlequin wedding dress would make your wedding day special. Mail via first-class mail to: Harlequin Walk Down the Aisle Contest 1197, (in the U.S.) P.O. Box 9076, 3010 Walden Avenue, Buffalo, NY 14269-9076, (in Canada) P.O. Box 637, Fort Erie, Ontario L2A 5X3, Canada.

   Limit one entry per person, household address and e-mail address. Online and/or mailed entries received from persons residing in geographic areas in which Internet entry is not permissible will be disqualified.

3. Contests will be judged by a panel of members of the Harlequin editorial, marketing and public relations staff based on the following criteria:

   - Originality and Creativity—50%
   - Emotionally Compelling—25%
   - Sincerity—25%

   In the event of a tie, duplicate prizes will be awarded. Decisions of the judges are final.

4. All entries become the property of Torstar Corp. and will not be returned. No responsibility is assumed for lost, late, illegible, incomplete, inaccurate, nondelivered or misdirected mail or misdirected e-mail, for technical, hardware or software failures of any kind, lost or unavailable network connections, or failed, incomplete, garbled or delayed computer transmission or any human error which may occur in the receipt or processing of the entries in this Contest.

5. Contest open only to residents of the U.S. (except Puerto Rico) and Canada, who are 18 years of age or older, and is void wherever prohibited by law; all applicable laws and regulations apply. Any litigation within the Province of Quebec respecting the conduct or organization of a publicity contest may be submitted to the Régie des alcools, des courses et des jeux for a ruling. Any litigation respecting the awarding of a prize may be submitted to the Régie des alcools, des courses et des jeux only for the purpose of helping the parties reach a settlement. Employees and immediate family members of Torstar Corp. and D. L. Blair, Inc., their affiliates, subsidiaries and all other agencies, entities and persons connected with the use, marketing or conduct of this Contest are not eligible to enter. Taxes on prizes are the sole responsibility of winners. Acceptance of any prize offered constitutes permission to use winner's name, photograph or other likeness for the purposes of advertising, trade and promotion on behalf of Torstar Corp., its affiliates and subsidiaries without further compensation to the winner, unless prohibited by law.

6. Winners will be determined no later than November 15, 2001, and will be notified by mail. Winners will be required to sign and return an Affidavit of Eligibility form within 15 days after winner notification. Noncompliance within that time period may result in disqualification and an alternative winner may be selected. Winners of trip must execute a Release of Liability prior to ticketing and must possess required travel documents (e.g. passport, photo ID) where applicable. Trip must be completed by November 2002. No substitution of prize permitted by winner. Torstar Corp. and D. L. Blair, Inc., their parents, affiliates, and subsidiaries are not responsible for errors in printing or electronic presentation of Contest, entries and/or game pieces. In the event of printing or other errors which may result in unintended prize values or duplication of prizes, all affected game pieces or entries shall be null and void. If for any reason the Internet portion of the Contest is not capable of running as planned, including infection by computer virus, bugs, tampering, unauthorized intervention, fraud, technical failures, or any other causes beyond the control of Torstar Corp. which corrupt or affect the administration, secrecy, fairness, integrity or proper conduct of the Contest, Torstar Corp. reserves the right, at its sole discretion, to disqualify any individual who tampers with the entry process and to cancel, terminate, modify or suspend the Contest or the Internet portion thereof. In the event of a dispute regarding an online entry, the entry will be deemed submitted by the authorized holder of the e-mail account submitted at the time of entry. Authorized account holder is defined as the natural person who is assigned to an e-mail address by an Internet access provider, online service provider or other organization that is responsible for arranging e-mail address for the domain associated with the submitted e-mail address. **Purchase or acceptance of a product offer does not improve your chances of winning.**

7. Prizes: (1) Grand Prize—A Harlequin wedding dress (approximate retail value: $3,500) and a 5-night/6-day honeymoon trip to Maui, HI, including round-trip air transportation provided by Maui Visitors Bureau from Los Angeles International Airport (winner is responsible for transportation to and from Los Angeles International Airport) and a Harlequin Romance Package, including hotel accomodations (double occupancy) at the Hyatt Regency Maui Resort and Spa, dinner for (2) two at Swan Court, a sunset sail on Kiele V and a spa treatment for the winner (approximate retail value: $4,000); (5) Five runner-up prizes of a $1000 gift certificate to selected retail outlets to be determined by Sponsor (retail value $1000 ea.). Prizes consist of only those items listed as part of the prize. Limit one prize per person. All prizes are valued in U.S. currency.

8. For a list of winners (available after December 17, 2001) send a self-addressed, stamped envelope to: Harlequin Walk Down the Aisle Contest 1197 Winners, P.O. Box 4200 Blair, NE 68009-4200 or you may access the www.eHarlequin.com Web site through January 15, 2002.

Contest sponsored by Torstar Corp., P.O. Box 9042, Buffalo, NY 14269-9042, U.S.A.

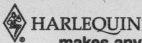

HARLEQUIN *Presents*

Passion™

Looking for stories that **sizzle**?

Wanting a read that has a little extra **spice**?

Harlequin Presents® is thrilled to bring you romances that turn up the **heat!**

Every other month there'll be a
PRESENTS PASSION™
book by one of your favorite authors.

Don't miss
THE ARABIAN MISTRESS
by **Lynne Graham**
On-sale June 2001, Harlequin Presents® #2182

and look out for
THE HOT-BLOODED GROOM
by **Emma Darcy**
On-sale August 2001, Harlequin Presents® #2195

Pick up a **PRESENTS PASSION**™ novel—
where **seduction** is guaranteed!

Available wherever Harlequin books are sold.

HARLEQUIN®
Makes any time special ®